THE NEW BIZARRO AUTHOR SERIES
PRESENTS

I0566359

THE
LITTLE
PUNK
PRINCESS

SARAH KARASEK

ERASERHEAD PRESS
PORTLAND, OREGON

ERASERHEAD PRESS
P.O. BOX 10065
PORTLAND, OR 97296

www.eraserheadpress.com
facebook/eraserheadpress

ISBN: 978-1-62105-294-4
Copyright © 2019 by Sarah Karasek
Cover design copyright © 2019 Eraserhead Press

Printed in the USA.

Chapter 1
Rare Moments

Once upon a time, there was a beautiful little princess whose chubby little cheeks were pinched by every celebrity, politician, and otherwise public figure she encountered; generally not for their cuteness, but as punishment for being so chubby. Her parents, the People In Charge, Mr. and Mrs. Walton-Clinton-Trump, entered her in every child beauty pageant, and she would have won even if the PIC hadn't instilled knee-knocking terror in every judge. In fact, she was so lovely, she would have won even if they had allowed her to appear without makeup and singing d-beat instead of disco-pop. She was spoiled beyond Rancid (whom she enjoyed in rare moments of respite from supervision) in preparation for the day she would rule the ruling class. So spoiled was she that she would have been called Princess even if her parents hadn't named her such.

Princess lived in the land of America, The America. It wasn't a very big land, but she didn't know that. What she had heard from the grumblings of commoners was that she lived in a swamp, but having never learned anything about ecology, she could only assume that a swamp was synonymous with the green glow of the riverbeds at night or perhaps the great wide roads branching out from the Gold House through the middle-class neighborhoods that surrounded it.

As Princess grew into puberty and her hormones went wonky, causing her to believe all sorts of crazy things, such as the shittiness of pop music and the oppression of youth, she began to explore those broad streets. She couldn't get away from the supervision of bodyguards at first, but soon she found that if she simply told them she had to change a tampon, she could sneak out a bathroom window and roam for hours without suspicion. Quite secretly, for she quickly discovered she'd be harshly punished if caught, Princess gathered heavy metal, punk, and ska tapes and CDs on these excursions from out of dumpsters and the occasional speakeasy (although she rarely ventured far enough from the upper-middle-class homes to find these). She'd discovered that the lazy lower-middle class simply didn't have enough self-respect or work ethic to prevent their roads from narrowing and developing gaping holes. Only once had a guard questioned the wreak of garbage emanating from her, to which she simply replied, "Very expensive, top-of-the-line perfume. Do you like it?" He'd nodded solemnly.

After a bit more experience, Princess further expanded her collection by sneaking into the confiscation vaults just outside the House. From these, she discovered hair metal, folk metal, horror punk, and industrial. She stashed all these carefully away in the few uninspected crannies of her room, all the while fantasizing about the pirates of old who stole such illegal music from the internet, but she knew better than to try herself. Long ago, the PIC had purchased the internet and employed a team of magicians to prevent the sharing of "deviltry, deviance, and discord" over the web. They monitored these things heavily.

But as she approached the age of eighteen, such taste had been almost completely cleansed from her soul. Years of being subjected to soap operas, pop music, reality television, and The News wore her down. Although she never quite grew to like these things—she especially detested The News, a strange amalgamation of State-appointed-celebrity life, the scandals and slandering of lesser politicians, and sanctioned fashion tips—they had a certain mind-numbing effect that caused her to care less and less about the words of Gogol Bordello, the riffage of Amorphis, and the beats of the Beastie Boys.

However, while Princess's musical urges progressed to a dull top 40s list, her chubbiness simply would not be suppressed. By the age of eighteen, she resembled Aphrodite of Knidos more than the ancient Idol of Twiggy. The PIC tried everything they could think of (although they weren't a very intelligent couple, so they asked their advisors as well), but nothing seemed to work. Despite the dozens of flights of stairs up the Eastern Gold Tower to Princess's room, all carpeted with the luscious furs of snow leopards and South

China tigers, animals otherwise restricted to legend, Princess continued to retain muscle mass. No matter how few calories she consumed, no matter how much celery she ate, her waist remained a healthy 34 inches.

The first six months of her State-sanctioned adulthood went on like this as she settled into the dullness of her fate, the dullness only interrupted by the trying of new fad diets. She was eating dinner on such a diet when her fate began to change, although whether or not this particular dinner determined her fate is debatable.

Mr. Walton-Clinton-Trump In Charge sat in the casual dining hall in his usual seat at the head of a long mahogany table, wearing a specially tailored suit and devouring a plate full of greasy burgers and heavily processed fish sticks. To his left sat Mrs. Walton-Clinton-Trump In Charge in a slim-fitting red dress with CD-sized hoop earrings made of solid gold. She nibbled daintily on a bowl full of ketchup and croutons and occasionally fluttered her long fake eyelashes. Princess sat to her father's right, playing some mindless game on her phone. She'd finished her three slices of cucumber and spoonful of raw egg white many minutes earlier. The whole family was identically spray-tanned.

Princess glanced up from her phone, and noticing all the servers had left the room, asked her father if she might have a second helping of cucumber slices. Mr. PIC quickly shushed her of course, fearing the caterers might overhear and feed this spat to the tabloids. He glanced about the long dining hall as if the silk-screened tapestries themselves, all depicting him in various heroic poses, might reveal this great embarrassment. Mrs. PIC shook her head patiently and batted her two-inch-long lashes, saying, "No my dear, but a second helping of celery couldn't hurt."

Her father rang for Princess's personal maid to return and demanded his daughter get another plate, this one holding two sticks of celery, but when the maid saw Princess's starving, dejected (yet uncomfortably haughty) face, she took pity on the girl. When she returned with the plate, she managed to slip a cherry tomato under the table into Princess's lap with deft, work-calloused hands. Princess nodded her usual TV-camera thank you smile, although whether she was hiding her gratitude from her parents or merely ungrateful is a matter of dispute.

Regardless, after Princess had eaten her celery (and slipped the forbidden fruit into her mouth during an obnoxiously fake coughing fit), she excused herself from the dinner table under the pretense of catching the beginning of "Naked Bachelorette Makeover" (although she secretly wished to hear a bit of Twisted Sister). Unfortunately, Liberty, the Head of Big Fashion had chosen today to dress her in the whitest and holiest of mini-shorts, so that as she stood to leave, a pinkish stain from the tomato became visible on her hip.

Mrs. Walton-Clinton-Trump screamed in horror and conveniently fainted, but Mr. Walton-Clinton-Trump, in a sudden onset of intelligence, realized that the stain must have been created by a sort of food. With Ferrari-like speed, he not only fired every member of the catering staff and set in motion their deportation, but also called an emergency meeting among his closest advisors (the Heads of Big Oil, Big Military, Big Pharmacy, and all the other Big Heads). As is the custom in such stories, Princess was sent to and locked in her room at the highest point of the Gold House.

Hours later, long after Princess's trek up her dozens of flights of stairs, she sat, or rather reclined, on her bed (the mattress of which was rather heavy from the gold shavings sprinkled throughout—an advisement from both the Big Head of Fashion and the Big Head of Alchemy, who had said respectively that it was both "all the rage" and a way to "clear her head of impure inclinations"), listening to "I Wanna Rock" at a very high volume through a single earphone. Despite the very high volume, she heard a slight knock at her door, which may have been not so slight due to that high volume.

Regardless, Princess shouted, "Come in!" quite haughtily, quickly turned her MP3 player off, and stashed it under her mattress.

Juanita, the kindly maid whose name Princess would have known had she possessed an inkling of compassion, appeared in the doorway as Princess pressed the green button to open the door. She entered quietly and began in tones strangely lacking in reverence, "Princess, they'll skin my hide for this, but I've known you since birth—"

"Don't bring up such embarrassing times!" Princess interrupted.

Juanita quietly shut the door behind her, did something akin to rolling her eyes which Princess either missed or overlooked, and continued. "You surely can't imagine that over all these years of cleaning your rooms that I've never noticed your Agent Orange or Ramones CDs, your Tank tapes… And yet you're the heiress to this king- Presidency," Juanita caught herself before letting the profane word slip out.

Princess stroked her hair and narrowed her eyes before finally saying, "I will not be blackmailed. A thousand dollars should solve this."

Juanita laughed. "You misunderstand. You may be the heiress of the country richest in dollars," and she paused here worrying she'd go too far, "but this is also a country lacking in culture—the culture I know you crave. The metal, the punk, all of it." She slowly reached into her pocket as Princess slowly processed this. Pulling out a worn rectangle of paper, she said, "I can't leave this estate without giving you a way to explore. This is a passport."

Princess ripped it from her hand. "What is this?" she demanded, then looked at it. It had all the fonts and colors of a carnival ticket. In fact, written in large black letters, it specifically read, "Carnival." Princess read the fine print aloud, "New Mexico? You give me a passport to an uncivilized land with a failed economy? A tiny speck on the map compared to my great country!"

Despite the outburst, Juanita caught the glimpse of curiosity in Princess's eyes. She bowed her head. "As you know, I've been banished. This is the only way I can help you now. Please think about it. If you change your mind, head south to The Wall." Then she opened the door and left the room.

As the door shut behind her, she thought to herself, "All Existing Universe, please restore this child's ability to think."

$$$

Meanwhile, Mr. PIC sat dozing in his gold leather chair at the head of yet another long rectangular table. This one, however, was located in his cabinet conference room. Appropriately, the walls were lined with cabinets, mostly full of documents he'd signed and never glanced at again. Others contained documents the PICs of yore had signed and, most likely, never glanced at again, except possibly to have them destroyed. The cabinets made the room feel a bit like a storage closet, and in response, the Big Head of Interior Design had insisted on the floor being painted a smattering of pastels, which were accentuated by the fluorescent lights overhead. They had been discussing the problem of Princess's weight again.

After hours of deliberation and dozens of PowerPoint slides, the Big Fashion Head suddenly remembered something. "Mr. Person In Charge," she squawked from under her Saturn-inspired sun bonnet. The rings stuck out so far that she had had to pump up her wheely chair to full height so that now they hung droopily over the Heads of Big Pharma and Big Necromancy, who were seated on either side of her. After she had properly awoken him, she continued, "The other day, I was reviewing potential articles for Black Magic Beauty—BMB, you know, my newest up-and-coming web-reality-travel-- "

"Of course, of course, go on."

"Well, I assumed it was total hogwash, so I didn't select it, but there was an article about a certain personal trainer magi who seemed just too good to be true, supposed to work wonders really, and it might be going out on a limb, but a thin, sexy limb, and you are really the very first I've told this to. You're quite in the know right now, Mr. Person In Charge. Not to say that you aren't usually, but it's really very exciting stuff. I would be just thrilled if I were you, being told this by me! First to hear it from - "

"Very good, Ms. Big Fashion Head! I thought you knew we were looking for every possible cure though, any treatment that could help overcome this… limitation."

For a moment, the room was still with anticipation for all the drama of a good firing, but when that moment ended Mr. Walton-Clinton-Trump was overtaken by an uncharacteristic onslaught of something like pity or appreciation. He displayed a glittering smile and declared, "Ms. Big Fashion Head, I've just had the most titanic idea!" And before anyone could even consider the consequences of pointing out this refashioning of events, he continued, "There's a certain personal trainer magi who has come to my attention through, through, my knowing of all things." He flashed his brilliant teeth again, as if there were a camera in the far right corner of the room, or perhaps at the coral bust of himself that sat there. "I would like for you to contact his person and have them summoned immediately to attend to my Princess!"

"Right away, Mr. Person In Charge!" she said, lowering her chair in preparation to leave.

"And however much the magi asks for, tell it I will pay half that. I trust you know how to make a deal!"

Chapter 2
The Hole in the Wall

Princess tossed and turned, unable to sleep with the guilt of eating that tomato and the usual rumbling in her stomach. Finally, she spread her legs and quietly rubbed her clit, imagining the most erotic thing she could think of. Although it started with one of the innumerable sex scenes she'd seen in the soap operas, it soon shifted to a skinny version of herself. By the time she climaxed, she was imagining that skinny version of herself on stage, every orifice filled with drum sticks, while the heavy metal band, Fist Fiend, played from somewhere she couldn't see. She drifted off to sleep.

She dreamt of a horrifying carnival where no money was accepted, so she could not buy her prizes, so that no matter what she did, she couldn't get any prizes at all. The clowns were terrorists, having attempted to infiltrate the media or create universal healthcare. The one at the dunk tank hollered, "America, Inc. is no better than any other country!" And worst of all, the carousel played heavy metal… and she liked it.

She awoke to the sound of her door buzzer, haunted by that memory. Her nose was stuffy with Valium, stolen from her mother, stolen from her father, who'd had the police steal it from a terroristic drug dealer whom he'd promptly had executed. The War on Drugs was real.

She reached to the red button that would allow her visitor to speak and promptly began to dress. Thong, leggings, bra, low-cut shirt with one of Mr. PIC's favored brands plastered across her breasts. If she would truly be heiress to the Presidency, she'd need enhancements in the next year or so.

"You have a special meeting today!" her mother's voice sang through the loud speaker, "Today is the day you'll discover how to be beautiful! Open up!"

Princess cast a glance around her room to make sure all her musical paraphernalia was hidden and then pressed the green button to open the door. Her mother strutted in, wearing a tight-fitting dress cut down almost to her belly button and a necklace hanging down to her crotch, bearing the sign of the cross with an elephant on the right and a donkey on the left. Around the animals and cross was a rectangle, as there always was in donkephant imagery, to symbolize how the two parties kept all goodness within their range (while evil prevailed outside the box). All she knew about the cross was that it was some ancient symbol from her country's history.

"Yes, mother?" Princess asked in tones both meek and sultry. "Who might my visitor be?"

"None other than Grand Mage Voguelle. The rage of all the fashion magazines. Wear something nice. He'll be discussing a plan to cure your… limitations."

Were she not so well trained, Princess would have clenched her fists and teeth, but instead she showcased her perfect pearly whites in the way she'd been taught to greet the opposing party, whichever side of the donkephant that might be at a particular campaigning season, and said, "Of course mother, I'll have The Head of Big Fashion pick out something special immediately. What time should I be ready by?"

"Eight of course, dear. He'll be dining with us. I'd like to have tested the new serving staff a bit more first, but so is the way of… you know. Which reminds me, your new maid is Victoria. She might introduce herself as some unpronounceable jumble of sounds. If so, please remind her of her new name. But if it happens again, notify me immediately. She'll be here at five sharp."

"Yes, mother."

"Is something wrong? You don't sound as… proud as usual. Fix that before you meet Voguelle."

"I'm just concerned that Victoria won't fluff my pillows properly," Princess lied.

Mrs. PIC nodded solemnly. "As am I, but your father assures me that Household Security has vetted these people with the tightest screening and the toughest vetting."

"Then it must be true. Thank you, mother. And please thank father for me."

"Of course. I'll see you fashionably around 8pm in the Golden Dining Hall." She left and the door closed and locked automatically behind her.

Princess stood up and looked around her room, which was impeccably clean aside from a pile of clothes from the previous day and her unmade bed, as if with x-ray vision: her MP3 player under her mattress, her tape deck in the carefully carved out hollow of a pile of Cosmo magazines sitting on the end table between her couch and television, the hoard of tapes and CDs hidden in the hole in the wall behind Mr. PIC's portrait, her childhood. Apparently so badly hidden Juanita had found all of it. She sighed. She could destroy it all herself now or wait for Victoria to find it. Unless Victoria was like Juanita, a terrorist technically, then her parents would have it destroyed and she'd get a harsh talking to, get grounded, and be forced to watch The News for months.

Then Princess's x-ray vision caught the ticket to New Mexico, temporarily hidden in a 3-month-old pair of gym socks (not new enough that Big Fashion would ever dress her in them, but not so old that they'd be thrown out to fill the land either). Her pink clock said thirteen after one. Slowly, Princess retrieved her MP3 player, placed an earphone in her ear, and played "We're Not Gonna Take It."

$$$

The knock came at precisely 5pm. Princess flipped the television on and caught a few seconds of The News (a woman running for Congress had been caught having pre-marital sex and they had the exclusive footage) before pressing the green button to open her door. Victoria was a short, stocky blonde woman and she curtsied before entering. "A pleasure to meet you," she said. "I am your new maid, Victoria. May I call you "Princess" or would you prefer something else?"

Yesterday, Victoria had been Hildegarde Luxemburg who lived in the slums where she taught grammar. It was a passion of hers. She believed slang was abhorrent and would happily beat it out of the young and reckless. In the evenings and on the weekends, she'd venture from the slums to the mansions of the upper-middle class (some of her students called this the upper class, but she corrected them vehemently), where she'd cook or clean or organize their homes. She'd acquired an impressive reputation of never leaking a single secret, always washing the dirty laundry before even thinking of airing it. Now here she was, in the Gold House, with room and board and a few extra dollars for luxuries, all for the small price of changing her name to Victoria. She was determined to surpass the woman she replaced in every way.

Princess eyed her suspiciously. "Didn't anyone give you any instructions on how to address me?" she said finally.

"Regretfully, I was not given any specific instructions on this particular matter. I was only told that the previous maid referred to you as Princess."

"I guess that'll do then. Come in." Princess glanced around her room one final time for any illegal media.

Victoria pushed her cleaning cart in and began by gathering the pile of dirty laundry that had accumulated since Juanita's departure yesterday. After this, she began to dust. Princess stared at the television and watched Victoria clean, trying to glean some hint of her character. She wasn't sure which was more boring.

It wasn't until Victoria lifted the photograph of Mr. PIC off the wall that she gleaned anything. Firstly, The News was far more boring. Secondly, the new maid handled surprises very well.

Before reacting in any visible way at all, Victoria thoroughly dusted the picture and replaced it on the wall. Then she turned around and said in professional tones, "Princess, I'm sorry this had to happen on our first day, but I must report this to your father immediately. I'm sure you understand that I am very loyal to your family, including yourself, but your father certainly knows best."

Princess's hand fidgeted over the couch cushion covering her MP3 player. "Of course."

As Victoria walked out the door, she could barely suppress the broad smile that threatened to sweep the stern wrinkles right off her face. Surely she would be honored; for her discreetness, if not her discovery.

Princess stood up and, before she realized what she was doing, punched a hole through her father's face. Just above his suit, where her fist had flown, her tapes and CDs peeked through the portrait. In her delirious state, it looked like an album cover to her. In ten minutes, the contents of the hole were in her backpack along with a little black dress so old Big Fashion would never notice it was gone, a large floppy hat from last season, a stylish pair of sunglasses, and a few womanly necessities. In her back pocket was the passport to New Mexico. It was in her back pocket because her hand seemed to tingle every time she touched it. Before placing it there, she'd examined it more closely and realized it featured a very artistic map drawn on the back from the southern gate of The Wall to a dot labeled "The Stage." Princess hoped she could find that gate.

Certain that Victoria had not been granted an audience with her very busy father so quickly, he was preparing for the Grand Mage Voguelle after all, Princess strode confidently down the stairs of her tower. If questioned, she'd simply explain she was trying to lose a bit more weight before meeting their guest. That was sure to embarrass any inquirers from further questions.

She was a bit more careful when she reached the main portion of the Gold House, for she was supposed to be grounded. Her pockets were lined with dollars and gold and gold-plated dollars in case she ran into any trouble, but she stuck to areas without security cameras, especially those areas the Grand Mage was unlikely to see, and only ran into five of her parents' regular attendants, none of whom questioned her.

She left the House through the glittery, golden main doors and followed the familiar route she'd used when leaving to search dumpsters for bits of her music collection. It wound through fancifully trimmed ornamental bushes, mostly in the shape of one or both of her parents, but there was the occasional eagle, and gardens of various red and blue flowers. When she had left the grounds and began walking past modest, upper-middle-class mansions, she took a deep breath. The cameras here were watched far less frequently than those in the House, and if she merely showed off her identity enough, people would trip over themselves trying to help her. She'd walked three blocks (she wasn't sure in what direction) when a long black car with tinted windows and the official valet insignia pulled up beside her. He rolled down his window. She hadn't the least clue what his name was, but he'd driven her places before.

"Might I be of assistance?" he called once she acknowledged him.

"Yes, actually," she said, approaching the car. He swiftly put it in park and ran out to open the door for her as she continued, "I feel like traveling south today. Do you know anywhere suitable for me to make an appearance among the people?"

The valet was briefly confused, for she'd been walking due north, but quickly began to wrack his brain for an appropriate location. No fine dining today, but a place where perhaps one or two slummers might be found among the middle class, blowing a holiday bonus or a lucky gambling streak. No more than one or two. And she'd surely only want to get something small, maybe only a sparkling water, but he couldn't act like he'd assumed.

"What're you in the mood for today, Miss Walton-Clinton-Trump?" he asked as he took the first right turn.

This rebellious streak brought images of greasy burgers and pizzas dripping in cheese to her mind, but she took the safe route and said, "A salad."

"I know the perfect place," he said, making the second right to get them heading south.

The drive was less quiet than normal, the valet thought. Princess asked questions about the neighborhoods, about how the lower-middle class (as she called them) got along with the upper-middle class (as she called them) in the particular area. He assured her she'd be quite secure, noting silently her lack of bodyguards. He wondered if she was preparing to campaign. After forty minutes of similar questions and some nearly genuine conversation, he parked the car in front of an all-American diner.

"Valet?" Princess said. He turned around to look at her. "Do you have a family?" She'd seen her father conduct business this way a number of times.

"I have my mother. She's a sweet old thing," he said, very confused now.

Princess reached into a pocket and pulled out three gold-plated dollars. "Buy her something nice," she said and, after what she hoped was an appropriately long pause, added, "Don't worry about picking me up, I'll make my own way back." Then she opened her own door (after a bit of fumbling with the safety lock) and walked into the diner.

The valet sat dumb-founded for a minute, weighed his small fortune on the scale installed in every valid valet car, then headed straight to his mother's house with the hopes that she hadn't died in the six months since he'd seen her last.

Princess watched him pull away through the restaurant window. She had already ignored the "Please wait to be seated" sign and placed herself in a corner where she hoped she might spot any guards or politicians before they spotted her. The diner was about what she expected, somewhere around a fifty-person capacity with a red-white-and-blue theme. Most of the customers were dressed fashionably, although some were a season or two behind. A couple three tables over from her were clearly from the lower-middle class though. Their sneakers had dirt on them, she had a pimple on her forehead, and his shirt didn't even have a brand name on it. She'd have to find a way to talk to them, but she knew that if she sat too close, the lower-middle class had a tendency to flee.

When the waitress came over, she ordered a sparkling water and a small fry. Why not splurge a little? The waitress seemed surprised, but Princess was sure that a bribe similar to the one she'd given the valet would work on this woman as well.

Princess sipped her sparkling water, waiting for the couple to leave and hoping that she could follow them to somewhere more private. Just minutes after she devoured her fries, they did leave and Princess hurriedly sat a $50 tip on the table and rose to follow them. It was a bit difficult for her to keep up with their fast, working-class pace in her high heels, but she managed to go twelve blocks to a rather decrepit apartment where the couple paused. She glanced up and down the street for police or paparazzi, and seeing none, quickly confronted them before they could enter.

"I'd like your assistance," she said, without realizing the menacing quality of her tone or statement. She watched their fight-or-flight instincts engage, but they swiftly moved past them, as good citizens should, and stood in front of their slightly ajar and very dirty door with mouths hanging open.

Princess recognized a skunky smell emanating from their apartment, from a few occasions she had walked past the facilities of the Federal Drug Enforcement Bureau. She thought it best not to mention it. Glancing around the street again, she reached into her pocket, palming a $100 bill, before extending her hand and saying, "Hi, I'm Princess." It was another trick she'd learned from her father. Once the woman grasped her hand, she continued, "But neither of you ever saw me here and especially did not tell me how to get to the south gate undetected." The woman took the bill, gave the man she was with an astonished glance, then fervently nodded.

"Best to stick to the well-lit streets, those ones are most supervised by police and such," the man said. At first, Princess thought he had utterly missed her point, but he continued, "If you were to continue down this unsavory street, you'd find a shady alley to your left. Best to avoid that alley, and whatever you do, not to cry 'Help!' when you reach the gaping pothole a few blocks down."

Princess smiled in bemusement. What strange systems the lower-middle class had. She slipped a fifty into her hand and shook the man's hand somewhat emphatically. Then she set off, but not before asking the couple if they had any hand sanitizer. They did not.

As Princess entered the shady alley, her heart began to race, and despite herself, she noticed her skin began to feel as if she'd just stepped out of a hot tub on a cool night. She resolved to apply more deodorant in her next moment of privacy.

Not only was there no sidewalk here, barely enough space for a small car to fit through in fact, but the pavement, if you could call it that, was clearly not designed with high heels in mind. After passing any number of potholes that could have been called 'gaping,' she finally came across one that took up nearly the entire road. She took a deep breath (in which she briefly considered that her musical addiction had actually warped her mind, that she was doing something incredibly stupid, that she'd have to spend all of her bribe money to get her out of it, and that she ought to return to the Gold House immediately and prepare to meet the Grand Mage Voguelle) then shouted, "Help!" The thought of another diet, of more reality shows, was just too much for her.

There was an uncomfortably long pause in which nothing happened. At first, Princess had the unsettling feeling that she was being watched, but that gave way to an even more unsettling feeling that she had been tricked and everyone was laughing at her now. Then a small door opened next to her and a very hunched-over woman said, from behind a set of iron bars that most doors and windows in this area had, "What's that you say?"

"Help?" Princess asked.

The old woman narrowed her eyes and glanced up and down the alley. Then she unlocked the iron bars, stepped outside, and looked up at the sky. Satisfied that there was no immediate threat, she opened the door further and beckoned Princess inside. Princess noted that her saggy tits weren't uplifted by any sort of bra, very obviously, and attributed at least part of the paranoia to that.

She fought past her revolt at the elderly woman's wrinkly face and gnarled hands—all the old women she'd ever met were pumped full of botox—and obeyed. The door shut swiftly behind her and Princess found herself standing in a small foyer, lit dimly by a few candles. The candles made her even more curious than the strange scent—something like the spice closet in the kitchen at the Gold House, a bit of that skunk smell she'd noticed from the couple's apartment, and just a hint of liquor shelf and cat litter—because candles were highly unpatriotic and even more inconvenient. They took money away from the hard workers at the power plants and the coal mines and the fracking companies, and the house fires they started were constantly in The News. Even Princess knew that.

The old woman noticed Princess's puzzlement and said in a gravelly voice, "They ward off phantoms and specters. I hope you ain't one."

"But what about the coal miners and the—" Princess wasn't used to being cut off but when the woman raised her hand, the calloused palms and protruding knuckles did the job.

"The whole industry, phantoms and specters. I imagine you've never worked a job like that," she said. "But more importantly, who might I be lecturing at the moment?"

Princess blinked then told the woman her first name, at which point the woman sighed and asked for her last name. Upon hearing her last name, the woman looked anxious and held out her hand expectantly. Princess fumbled around in her pockets until she found a $100 bill then placed it in her palm. At this, the woman spit on the floor and held the bill over one of the candles.

Princess gasped audibly and held back an urge to strike the woman, but the money took much longer to light than she had expected and she was feeling mostly fascinated when the old woman explained, "Your ticket to the carnival, child." Then she poured some sort of fluid on the bill impatiently and it went up in flames.

She cackled the whole while it burned then slipped into a fit of smoker's coughs as she examined the ticket.

When she'd finished coughing, she looked up at Princess's still bewildered face and explained, "Magic is everywhere. But here especially, you gotta make it for yourself." Princess didn't understand, but she nodded and the woman opened a door on Princess's left. She handed the ticket back to her and croaked, "Right this way then. Thelemita wouldn't want you crossing the pothole. Lucky you found me and not some other smuggler. I'm Marion, but you can call me Matilda or Ted, or perhaps, if you're feeling ballsy, ma'am."

"W-w-who? What?"

"Juanita. Of course, you know her as Juanita. Now might be a good time to don that disguise of yours by the way." The hallway was so dark that Princess could only see the silhouette of Marion from the candle she carried. Occasionally, a streak of light struck the darkness through what Princess imagined were boarded up windows. Nonetheless, something about this woman made Princess obey and she tripped along in her heels, digging through her purse with one hand, searching for the feel of her floppy hat and sunglasses. When Marion came to a halt, she nearly collided with her, but she put on her sunglasses just in time for a door to open into an incredibly bright room with the incredibly fetid smell of fecund soil.

When they'd stepped out, Marion locked the door behind her. Princess noticed three large key rings hanging from her overalls. Then she noticed the woman was eyeing her up and down with her head tilted in a way that caused her long, stringy white hair to look even thinner. "Wait here," she said, and rustled off into the rows of plants with unexpected speed. Within seconds she'd disappeared behind small trees and ferns and hanging baskets of herbs, none of which Princess could even pretend to identify, although she did notice some moss here and there.

The old woman returned minutes later - which was an awfully long wait for Princess, who was accustomed to spending such times playing games on her phone— appearing just as suddenly as she'd disappeared, with a small bundle of dried plants and a fistful of dry dirt. Before Princess could think, the old woman had thrown the dirt into the air so that Princess's designer clothes were now marred with brown stains. Marion shushed her like one might shush a finicky toy dog, then pulled a match from her pocket, which she struck against the knee of her overalls, and lit the plant bundle. She circled around Princess, humming something Princess thought she recognized.

Drawing the song into her working memory, Princess shouted, "Weirdwood! The Slow Poisoner!" The bundle was almost burnt down and Princess suddenly realized how content she'd been contemplating the tune.

Marion nodded. "Good decision Thelemita made. Where'd you find such a thing?"

Princess thought for a moment while Marion stubbed out the bundle. "Dumpster, just after a raid, a few blocks away."

The old woman sniffed Princess's shoulder and announced, "Perfect!"

"What was that?" Princess asked, worried her contentment meant she was high on some unknown substance, or possibly had been slowly poisoned.

"Dumpster," Marion muttered and replied, "Sage and tobacco, for cleansing and blending in. You smell like a cigarette and a number of unrecognized belief systems."

"You mean third parties?" Princess asked, feeling a certain kinship with the woman now over the shared music.

Marion shrugged. "Do you have sneakers?"

Princess nodded and fished around in her bag before finally pulling out a pair of Nikes with four-inch heels. She sat down on a nearby bench—well, a two-by-four laid across two buckets, but essentially a bench—and began to change into them. Marion shook her head and walked away.

When she came back, she was carrying a pair of brown boots, obviously very used. Princess had just finished putting on her sneakers. Marion said, "Wear those for now if you must, but bring these with you. Trust me, you'll be glad you did."

Princess sighed heavily. "I can't possibly fit those bulky things in here." And she thought to herself, "I can't possibly let those atrocious things get oil and mud all over my Gucci bag."

Marion shrugged again. "Then leave your heels here. Or perhaps use a backpack instead. Your shoulders will thank you." Princess imagined herself carrying some unbranded backpack and begrudgingly took her heels out of her bag.

"You can sell them if you want. At least $200 each, used," Princess said.

Ignoring the comment, the old woman asked, "I assume you've brought food and water?"

Princess shook her head. "I just had lunch."

"Oh, Thelemita, the things I do for you," Marion grumbled and left again. This time, she returned with a thermos and two paper baggies. She held up the thermos. "I've filled it up with water for you, but when you run out, you can fill it up yourself from just about anything. It'll filter all the harmful shit out and it should be good for another five or six filtrations." She tipped it upside down and something clacked against the side. "It won't spill and it has this clip you can hook to your purse." Then she held up the baggies. "This is beef jerky and this one is full of apple chips."

Princess realized she'd have to rework her whole way of eating, but she nodded.

"You should be ready then," Marion said. "Best get as much distance between yourself and that castle before anyone notices you're gone, and although I'm not quite sure what exactly you do as the heiress, I'm certain there are events scheduled for you throughout the day. Follow me." Princess stood up, immediately aware that her sneakers had not, in fact, made her feet feel much better than her heels had, and followed the old woman through the greenhouse. What she had first mistaken for bright sunlight, she now realized was the light of dozens of sun lamps. Like the hallway, this room had no windows, although most of the plants were lush enough and placed closely enough that it was difficult to spot walls.

$$$

Victoria had made it to a third waiting room. This one was smaller and much more intimate. The chairs were upholstered with red leather and the carpet felt softer under her shoes. There were only six chairs, as opposed to the thirty chairs in the first waiting room she'd been placed in. That first room had held fifteen people besides herself, some with a distinct touristy quality to their smiles, others who sat with the confidence of dignitaries, and still a few who wriggled nervously in their seats, obviously hoping to ask the People In Charge for some favor. Those people were the first to go. Some of the confident ones and even some of the tourists made it to the second room, where deep bass rhythms thrummed quietly in the background with occasional high-pitched vocals, consisting mostly of brand names and campaign slogans. Victoria found the grammatical structure rather enjoyable—a good balance of run-on sentences, fragments, and non-sequiturs were key, and of course, the exclusion of that slang the lower-middle class was so fond of. Victoria sat calmly next to a plastic fern, until a guide came and took the other occupants on a tour. Then she was quickly led to this third waiting room.

Although she'd initially been surprised that he hadn't gotten to speak with Mr. PIC sooner, given the grave subject matter, she supposed having only been able to relay to his secretary that she needed to discuss his daughter might account for the long wait. She was smoothing her knee-length black skirt when a door opened and a big man in a black suit gestured for her to follow him. She was led down a short hallway, which included many photographs of the Walton-Clinton-Trump family, and into a large office with a huge mahogany desk behind which Mr. Walton-Clinton-Trump In Charge himself sat.

"You asked for an audience with me?" he asked.

"In private, Mr. Person In Charge, please," Victoria said, glancing at the big man in the black suit.

Mr. PIC waved his hand around in a circular motion and the black-suited man promptly walked over to a corner and faced into it. "Continue." Nervously, Victoria pulled a pack of sticky notes and a silver sharpie from her apron and began to write. "Ah, silver, not a bad choice, although I prefer gold myself," Mr. PIC said. "Strongest metal there is."

Victoria handed him the note, which read: "Illegal media in your daughter's room. You certainly know better how to deal with it than me. Gold is a wonderful metal."

Mr. Walton-Clinton-Trump narrowed his eyes and leaned back in his chair. "Hugo!" he barked in the direction of the man in the corner. The man hesitantly turned around. His name tag read 'Bart,' but that didn't stop Mr. PIC. "Station yourself outside the door! And fix your badge immediately." The man silently left the room.

Mr. PIC fixed his gaze on Victoria and continued, "I trust your reputation is a true one and I am the first to hear of this." Victoria nodded, barely able to contain her excitement. "Did you confront Princess about this?"

Victoria nodded again and said, "Only briefly. I informed her I would speak with you about it at your soonest convenience."

"And where is this paraphernalia now?"

"I left it where it was. Couldn't risk someone seeing me leaving her quarters with it."

"Very good, Victoria. I'm going to text my wife. When she arrives, you can explain everything to her. The information will reach no further than the three of us. And perhaps one or two more individuals if necessary."

$$$

Princess followed Marion through a labyrinthine series of corridors, going deeper and deeper underground from what she could tell, although she based this solely off of the lack of sunlight. She didn't pay much attention to the fact that the floor felt very much like a sidewalk or that a small stream seemed to be running nearby. She'd ceased to be surprised by the myriad of strange smells in this part of her country, and so she also ignored the dull scent of human waste and river mud. After what seemed like hours, but Princess couldn't really tell (time was dragging without her cellphone) Marion handed her the little nub of her candle and climbed up a short ladder. There was a small landing at the top, just big enough that Marion could kneel. She lifted up the ceiling and peeked her head out. Yellow light came flooding into the tunnel and Princess was once again thankful for her sunglasses.

Marion looked down at Princess. "Climb up here. Quickly!"

Princess stared at the candle, at an utter loss, until Marion snapped her fingers and the flame went out. The rungs of the ladder weren't just cold, but gritty and a bit damp. She really wished she'd brought hand sanitizer. Marion helped her onto the landing once she made it to the top and then pulled her out into what appeared to be an empty kitchen.

"Where—" Princess began, but the old woman once again held up her bony hand.

Slowly and quietly, she lowered the floor back into place then straightened her back in a way that Princess hadn't imagined possible of the hunched old woman. Then she opened her mouth and the perfect replica of a crow's cry flew out into the building. Whoever was outside the room, Princess imagined customers eating dinner, servers serving, hushed perceptibly. Marion made the strange sound again. After a few seconds, she began to look frightened and bent to lift up the trap door.

Then, from just outside the kitchen doors to Princess's right, they heard the chittering of a squirrel. Marion sighed, silently but visibly, and stood back up. A short middle-aged man wearing flour-covered jeans, a black cut off, and an equally flour-covered apron hopped into the room, paused briefly, then ran to give Marion a hug. "Matilda, I've missed you!" he cried as loudly as he could in a whisper. Then he noticed Princess and gave her a deep bow, "Ms. Walton-Clinton-Trump In Charge, a pleasure to meet you," he said.

Marion cackled. "She's the package, Kai. Don't worry, it's fine."

"Oh." Kai looked flustered. "To?"

"Show him your ticket, dear," Marion said. Princess showed him. Marion added, "And with my blessing. She's found The Slow Poisoner, on her own." Then she added, even more quietly but still not below Princess's ability to hear, "Although she is a bit dull."

Kai glanced at the high-heeled sneakers and nodded. "I'll take care of her," he said. "Let you get back to your post. A pleasure to see you, as always."

Marion beamed, saluted Kai, and went back down the trap door. "Take care of yourself," she added, just before she shut it.

Kai turned back to Princess and said, "A wonder

that woman, a real wonder. Lucky you found her. Unfortunately, way the restaurant's running today, I'm gonna have to ask you to wait here 'til closing time. Real busy." Princess looked around and Kai held out his arms nonchalantly. "You can pose as a cook and help me chop things up or you can hide in the pantry, up to you. Got an extra apron over there." He gestured to the back of a chair in the corner. Princess wrinkled her nose involuntarily at the condition of the apron. "Best wait in the pantry then," Kai said. "Probably not much experience cooking anyway."

Princess followed him over to a door near the chair in the corner. Inside were buckets of fresh vegetables and jars of just slightly less fresh vegetables. It almost smelled like Marion's greenhouse. "You use all this?" Princess asked, astonished that some hole in the wall could get that much business.

"You don't need to know about that," Kai said. "But I'll have you know it doesn't go to waste." Then he began to shut the door and it began to grow very dark.

"Wait!" she said. "Aren't there any lights in here? How long until you close?"

"It'd be awfully strange if I kept the lights on in the pantry all the time. They'll have to stay off. We'll probably get ready in an hour or two. Don't worry though, I'll be in and out for supplies." Then he closed the door.

Princess could hear frying from some stove outside and the scent of steaks and potatoes drifted to her. Then new frying, evidently of bacon and eggs with more than a healthy serving of cheese. Her stomach growled and she decided to distract herself by trying to explore the room in the dark. She'd made it to the farthest corner and found something that seemed like it might serve as a seat when the door opened and Kai appeared again. "Told you I wouldn't be gone long," he said.

Princess took the chance to see what she was about to sit on and realized it was, in fact, shaped exactly like a recliner. Only it was a stack of cases of water and beer. She sat down carefully and spent some time listening to her music, before finally breaking down and eating some of the jerky. It was incredibly relaxing, knowing that she doesn't need to hide it. In what seemed like no time, Kai returned and ushered her out of the room. Princess had thought she would just waltz up in disguise and explain to the guards that she was leaving. After all, her father deported people all the time, it looked awfully easy to leave. However, at Kai's insistence (after informing her he would not help any other way), they crept through back alleys and avoided the Gate and the guards. Upon reaching The Wall, Kai pressed his back flat up against it and whispered for her to do the same. They shimmied along until they reached a huge pile of rubbish. Then they began to dig. In five minutes flat, they uncovered a hole in The Wall. Although it was only three feet at its widest, Princess climbed delicately through and found herself, for the first time ever, outside her country.

Chapter 3
Gatekeepers

Although it was darker outside The Wall than it was in the capital of The America, the sky was lit with searchlights roaming over the sand and cement. Princess kept Kai's warnings in mind—if she got caught in one of these, it would all be over. There was no bribing her way out of her father's will, he was far too rich for that. But she could see the moon in the sky, something she'd only ever seen on vacations to National Wildlife Hotels. Kai had told her the moon would be in the west, and she'd want to go south, so she ought to keep it to her right. She watched the searchlights, looking for some sort of pattern, then made a mad dash for a few hundred feet. She paused, out of breath, but nearly out of range, and laid down on the ground. Marion had already covered her clothing in dirt, it couldn't get much worse.

When she finally caught her breath and stood, a light just barely skimmed over her, but in a final dash, she made it out of range. Her feet were already killing her. Figuring no one would be seeing her anytime soon, she conceded and put on the hiking boots. They felt strange to her, but they were a bit more comfortable. After a half hour or so of trudging through sand, which was slowly becoming more and more like soil with more frequent patches of grass, she began to see flashes of light in the distance. Explosions in the sky. She worried there might be a battle raging ahead of her, but she had no idea where else to go and let her curiosity lead. As she got closer, she could hear people laughing. In fact, she could hear punk playing, just below the raucous laughter. There was a circle of small vehicles around the explosions and as Princess crept even closer, she could see a ring of at least thirty people sitting on blankets and kneeling against hoods. She could also feel a blade press lightly against her throat and hear a man's voice say, "Drop the bag and explain yourself." He led her into the circle.

Princess whimpered, "Please don't make me drop the bag. It's designer. You can take it from me, but the dirt—" Before she could finish, the man ripped the bag off her shoulder and lightly set it on the ground.

"Why're you here, poser?" he asked. A number of people from the part of the circle closest to her were watching now.

"Juanita," Princess began and suddenly realized she hadn't a clue as to this woman's last name. Grasping for any other signifiers, she added, "Thelemita."

"And how do we know you ain't a spy?" the man asked, although the blade moved a bit further from Princess's neck at the second name.

"I have a ticket to the carnival?" she asked.

The man laughed. "What's the third song off 3 Inches of Blood's 9th album?" he retorted.

"I...I don't know," Princess confessed. "I've only ever heard Goat Rider's Hoarde and Night Marauders."

From somewhere to her left, a low female voice shouted, "That band's shit anyway!" A number of people shushed her, but Princess could see some were nodding in agreement.

"Let's see you root the posers out then!" the man shouted into the darkness.

"What was the last song by The Creepshow that Hellcat sang in before giving birth?" the woman retorted.

Princess gulped. "No idea, honestly. I'm from—" The man cut her off again.

"We know where you're from. One more question. Who wants it? Then we take her to Hell's Spawn," the man with the knife said.

A person with liberty spikes approached. "I want the question," they said. They had a rather high-pitched voice, but Princess wasn't certain what their identity might be. They were close enough to her, and she was now lit up by torchlight for everyone to see, that she could read "Stormwomb Claw" across their shirt in almost illegibly archaic print. "What're your top three favorite songs by Fist Fiend?" they asked.

Princess breathed a sigh of relief. "The only album I was ever able to find by them was Wraith Squid Lies, but my favorite songs off that are definitely Necroslayer, Undead Elephant, and their cover of We're Not Gonna Take It."

"Looks like we're both escorting her to Hell's Spawn," the spiky-haired person said. Their voice took on a lower pitch now.

The knife man removed the blade from Princess's throat and they began walking out of the circle of small cars and towards the moon. "Keep up the celebrations!" he shouted over his shoulder.

"I really like Undead Elephant too," Princess's potential savior said. "Really wish we could resurrect them."

"The bass riffs are incredible," Princess said. "Can either of you tell me where we're going or is that some big secret?"

"Would you rather me or Occasum pat you down?" the knife man asked, ignoring the question.

"Excuse me?" Princess said.

"Can't have any weapons on you," Occasum replied.

"Wait, where's my purse?" Princess asked, suddenly remembering it.

"That where you put your weapons?" Knife-man laughed. "Or maybe you got it bugged."

"I'll have you know, I'm the daughter of Mr. Walton-Clinton-Trump In Charge. I'm certain if he wanted to send a spy, he'd pick someone a bit more low-key," Princess said.

"At the very least, looks like we got ourselves a bargaining chip," the knife man said to Princess's other escort. "If she's telling the truth anyway."

"I don't see why she'd be lying," said Occasum. "Awfully stupid thing to make up."

"Tell me where we're going!" Princess said.

"Not until we know you're not bugged. Just pat her down, Occasum. I can't deal with all this whining." Knife-man lit up a rolly and walked a few paces away.

"You'll tell me where we're going after this?" Princess asked. Occasum nodded, and Princess submitted to their instructions.

After about a minute, Occasum had finished and told Princess quietly, "Backstage." Then she shouted to the knife-man, who'd paced away a bit by now, "All clear, Sandworm." He snubbed out his cigarette, put the remainder behind his ear, and they resumed walking.

Princess was boiling over with excitement. Her hands were no longer being held behind her back, she was on her way to her destination, and although she couldn't be sure either of these two were to be trusted, she suddenly blurted out, "Juanita gave me this!" and handed her carnival ticket over to Occasum.

"It's the real deal," Occasum told Sandworm, examining it. She flipped it over, "It's even got Thelemita's handwriting on it." Then she handed it back to Princess.

Sandworm just shrugged. "We'll see what Hell's Spawn has to say."

They walked in relative silence for twenty or so minutes before reaching a vehicle like nothing Princess had ever seen. It was entirely plated in mirrors, except the windows, and had a huge metal thing, covered in wires, hanging out of the trunk. Anyone else would have guessed it was a make-shift battery. Under some of the mirrors, especially on top of the car, were an assortment of fans.

Occasum saw Princess's astonishment. "His baby, not mine," they said. "Has a weakness for early models. I'd call this one a prototype, personally."

"Get in," knife-man said. Occasum sat in the backseat next to Princess, to keep an eye on her no doubt. Sandworm started the car and a barrage of heated guitar riffage and double bass filled the vehicle.

Princess smiled and let her herself stare out the window. Sandworm drove slower than she was used to, which she thought at first was due to the bumpy terrain. Then he braked hard and Princess realized he was trying to avoid animals. Specifically rabbits. The ground was almost completely covered with grass now, except the patchiness on which Sandworm drove. And there were small trees appearing here and there, although sparsely. Princess was surprised how dark it was out here.

Half an hour later, Sandworm pulled the car into what had to be a parking lot, judging by the multitudes of other vehicles, although it was neither paved nor covered by a roof. There was a large building, what looked like an arena, nearby. A glowing sign hung from a pole in front of it, displaying in red text, "The Stage." The moment Sandworm turned the car off, Princess could hear that music was also blasting from this venue. She heard a trumpet wailing, along with a number of brass instruments she couldn't identify, the occasional scream of what sounded like an air horn, and the usual guitar, bass, and drums that she was used to. She thought it sounded like punk, but she wasn't quite sure. They all got out of the car. Then, over all the chaos, she heard the most beautiful female vocals her eardrums had ever been tickled by. Princess could only hear it faintly, but she was dying to let it vibrate her skull.

Occasum and Sandworm were staring at her. "Sounds like Swamp Slut," Sandworm grumbled.

Occasum nodded. "Gotta be. Come on, princess, not too far now. And Hell's Spawn isn't on stage, so we should be able to catch him pretty easy."

"Hell's Spawn?" Princess finally asked.

"It's hard to describe a legend," Occasum said. "You'll understand when you meet him."

As they walked on towards The Stage, Princess could see there were vines growing up the adobe walls (although she had no concept of adobe). When they reached the door, Occasum knocked three times and a hoarse voice shouted from the other side, "Weapons not food, not homes, not shoes, not need, just feed the war cannibal animal!"

Occasum shouted back, "I walk that corner to that rubble that used to be a library. Line up to that mind cemetery now!"

The door opened to a dirt-floored foyer. Sandworm mumbled, "Classic, too classic. You're slacking, Donna."

A tiny blonde woman in a ticket booth grinned at them. She was missing at least two teeth, no saying what condition her molars were in. "Not my fault you're no fan of classical poetry."

"Hey, Donna," Occasum said. "This one's got a ticket." They gestured for Princess to approach the booth.

Princess stepped forward readily enough but was concerned this strange woman would take her ticket and keep it. This was her passport. She reached into her back pocket and pulled the thing out but held it firmly in her hand. "Um, hi," she said. "This is my passport. And my map." She reached into another pocket to withdraw a bill but thought of Marion's reaction to her attempt. Finally, she handed the ticket to the tiny blonde.

Donna gave it a quick once-over, glanced at the back, and gasped. "Thelemita," she said. "She was always quite the artist." She handed it back and asked, "You know her?"

"Of course," Princess said. "She's my—was my maid."

"Do you know who this is?" Donna whispered.

"Of course," Occasum and Sandworm said in unison. Sandworm added, "The heir to tyranny and oppression."

Donna looked back to Princess, "If she sent you— How is she?"

"She's not here?" Princess asked. "She was deported yesterday." Donna turned to face the wall behind her.

"Come on," Sandworm said and pushed Princess to a door leading out of the foyer. The floor outside the foyer was also dirt. But it was much more outside. Princess could see the sky again and was shocked to see how clear it was. Not only could she see stars, but she could see dozens, maybe hundreds of them. She was standing on grass and moss.

"This is… nice," she said.

Occasum giggled. "Can't even imagine what it's like in The America by now. You mean the ground or the sky?"

"Both," Princess said. Sandworm was busy shouldering his way through a large crowd. The music was much louder here. Miss Walton-Clinton-Trump's heart was thumping. She'd never been in a crowd this big. Never been outside her country. Never heard vocals so penetrating.

"Can you make it through this, or do I need to drag you along?" Occasum asked. Princess suddenly realized that Sandworm was a few yards ahead of her now and Occasum was a few feet away and a number of people thrashing around wildly were threatening to break the chain. She nodded.

"I'll drag you along like some groupie then," they said.

"This music is great!" Princess shouted over a

trombone solo. She could see the band now and identify most of their instruments. She could also see that they were getting closer and closer to the strange construction of crates and pallets that the band was playing on.

"We're almost there, don't worry," Occasum shouted back. Suddenly Sandworm veered off to the left of the stage and Occasum, pulling Princess by the hand, veered just as quickly. In a few minutes they were standing in front of a bouncer who was standing in front of a door. The bouncer clearly recognized Sandworm and gave him a nod before stepping aside. The door was visibly heavy. Sandworm's rather large arm muscles tensed while pulling the thing open. It was also a few inches thick. The three of them entered a small hallway with three chairs on each side and a door at the other end. Occasum stopped partway down the hallway and, once Princess had also stopped, released her grip on Princess's hand.

Sandworm, however, continued straight down the hallway to the door. "Hey, Hell's Spawn, got a visitor for you."

A minute or two later, the door opened and a disheveled man in a gray t-shirt with at least three brown stains and four spiked bracelets appeared. He squinted down the hallway until his eyes landed on Princess, then he said, "Sandworm, my dude, here I thought you were bringing the party to me. I gotta be on stage in less than an hour but come on in for now. Always welcome to enjoy the show."

They walked into a room that Princess distinctly felt was a basement, although she knew they weren't underground. It had all the coolness, the humidity, the distance from what was going on outside. It was also painted entirely green, except for the floor, which was dirt. The disheveled man staggered around a set of floor toms and sat down on a black stool. Two bean bags and two lawn chairs sat on the other side, closest to the door. A small table near them held a dozen bottles of water (obviously glass, not plastic), a bottle of Vodka (also glass), and a large plate on which sat a few crackers and grapes. Sandworm sat on one of the lawn chairs and Occasum sat in a bean bag, leaving another bean bag between them. Princess chose the lawn chair next to Occasum. The man looked at the plate worriedly and said, "There's plenty more where that came from, if you're hungry."

"Thanks," Sandworm said. Occasum smiled. Princess's stomach growled. The man leaned forward and grabbed the plate, handing it to Princess. "Eat, stranger," he said. She took it and sat it on her lap, and politely nibbled a cracker. Then she stared pointedly at the floor. They were a little stale, but they were tasty.

"Hell's Spawn," Sandworm began.

"Stanislaus," the man said. "Call me Stanislaus when I'm not doing musical things." He reached out a hand to Princess. "Stanislaus Ramirez, and who might you be?"

"Princess Walton-Clinton-Trump," she said, then quickly added, "With a passport from Thelemita." She took his hand and shook it, after briefly wondering if she was supposed to stick money in it too.

"Princess Walton-Clinton-Trump With A Passport From Thelemita, a pleasure to meet you," Hell's Spawn said and chuckled. Princess realized he was ageless in a way she'd never seen. There were no signs of cosmetic surgery, possibly a bit of black hair dye and definitely a bit of eyeliner, but that's all. Yet she couldn't place him any better than somewhere between twenty-five and fifty. "I'm supposed to go to Backstage, sir," she said, feeling the need to pay this man reverence.

He spat on the dirt floor. "I won't hold it against you, since you're a newcomer," he said, "But never call me sir. It's insulting. Secondly, you're precisely at Backstage right now. May I examine your ticket?" Princess stood up so that she could take it from her back pocket and handed it to him. He examined it and said, "I hope your journey wasn't too rough?" handing it back to her.

"My feet are killing me," she said, lapsing into the traditional conversations she'd grown used to at the Gold House. She looked down, embarrassed, and found herself staring at the crackers and grapes. Quickly, rebelliously, she popped a grape into her mouth. "Thank you," she added, after she finished chewing.

"It appears she made most of the journey in heels," Sandworm said.

Stanislaus Ramirez nodded sadly. "Heels aren't the best footwear out here. Unless you're on stage, then they're rather acceptable." He gestured to his own raised pleather boots, then cleared his throat. "Why're you here, Princess?"

"I—Juanita—Thelemita gave me this and said it had something to do with the music I listen to. It's all illegal in The America. What I like anyway."

"But why did *you* come here?" he asked.

Princess thought for a moment, not on the importance of the question, but on her actual reasoning.

She felt strangely comfortable with Stanislaus, although she'd been quite nervous to meet Hell's Spawn. Then she thought back to that gaping pothole. "I'm sick of dieting," she said. "I don't want to meet the Grand Mage Voguelle. I don't care about the Top 40. And if I have to watch The News one more time, I swear—" she cut herself off. "And my new maid found my stash of propaganda and—she found my stash of music."

Hell's Spawn looked incredibly concerned. He took a deep breath and asked, "What do you listen to, Princess?"

"Illegal," she began, as if confessing to the Big Head of Anti-Anti-Patriotism. "Mostly punk and metal. I have this collection." She reached for her purse and realized she still didn't know it's location. "My collection is in my purse," she said, looking at Sandworm.

He shrugged. "It's your collection. You ought to know it."

"I listen to a lot of Twisted Sister, Tiger Army, Faith No More, The Specials. I really like Fist Fiend's Wraith Squid Lies, but I couldn't find any of their other albums."

Stanislaus nodded. "And what do you know about The Stage?"

"That band that's playing right now, they're amazing," Princess said. "That's all I really know."

Stanislaus smiled and nodded. "They're one of my favorites. I play with them every chance I get. You know, we can always do this later. Would you rather got out and mosh?"

"Mosh?" Princess asked.

"You'll see." Stanislaus chuckled, then sobered a bit looking at her clothes. "Would you like to change first, maybe? Have you brought another outfit?"

Princess glowered in Sandworm's direction. "I did actually, but it was in my purse, and I can't say I know the location of that right now."

Stanislaus raised his eyebrows at Sandworm, although continued to smile. "Would you care to get this newb's purse for her?" he asked.

"It's on its way here now," Sandworm said.

"Alright, well the least I can do then is to treat you to something from the Backstage closet. You can pick anything you want." Stanislaus stood and walked to a curtain behind him, which Princess assumed was covering a window. When he pulled the curtain back, it revealed loads of pleather pants and mini-skirts, long flowing gowns, anything imaginable in fishnet, and a few oddities that Princess couldn't even guess how to wear.

She gasped. Then after a few moments of no one making a move towards the closet, she asked hesitantly, "Pick it out myself?"

"Unless you're too chicken," Stanislaus said teasingly.

"But you don't have anything that'll fit me. I'm not thin like, like…" She looked around the room and at their confused faces. "I guess I'll give it a shot." She stood and approached the closet.

"I'm pretty sure there's something for everyone in there. These were all donated by people who grew out of them or people who got bored with them or people who just like making clothes and couldn't find homes for them," Stanislaus said reassuringly. Princess grimaced at the thought of wearing secondhand clothing, but was much too enthralled by the styles to care.

She was still sifting through the closet when a knock came at the door, although she had managed to set aside two pairs of black boots for contemplation. One was mid-rise and high-heeled and studded with silver stars. The other was knee-high, heeled like a hiking boot, and every inch of it was covered with straps, buckles, and snaps. A voice on the other side of the door said, "Yo, Stan Ram, fifteen minutes and we need Bleeding Empire on the stage, that includes Hell's Spawn."

"Have I ever been late for a show?" Stanislaus called. The voice laughed and Stan added, "Not having drank a 5th of vodka prior?"

"You have that bottle in there," the voice countered.

"I have three guests," Stanislaus said. "I'd never drink a whole 5th when I have three other people to share it with."

Princess spent the night standing awkwardly, then swaying slightly, then helicoptering her hair to Bleeding Empire. She'd chosen the more utilitarianly heeled boots, a white aluminum corset which fastened with the tabs from beer cans (but was lined with cotton), and a mid-thigh pair of green shorts sporting a dozen pockets. After the big show was over, a number of anybodies took the stage and made their own marvelous racket. The crowd thinned out then, mostly heading to bonfires outside The Stage and bars at its edges. Stanislaus Ramirez found Princess and gave her a tour of The Stage and Backstage, including a bit of their history and customs. The lack of money was specifically overwhelming to her.

Chapter 4
Squealing

After half an hour or so of discussing the matter Mr. and Mrs. Walton-Clinton-Trump In Charge rushed to the top of the gold tower with Victoria. Mrs. PIC knocked and called, "Princess dear, I'd like to speak with you." When there was no answer, she added, "We just need to talk, dear." She'd recently studied the lingo from a number of soap operas. After a few minutes, she tried the door, which swung open easily.

"Princess, your father and I are here," Mrs. PIC called to the empty room. After a few frantic minutes of the trio exploring, they realized that it was empty.

"Where is she?" thundered Mr. PIC. Victoria remained silent, hoping that by drawing no attention to herself, she wouldn't be blamed for this matter. Then, giving up, Mr. PIC asked her, "Where is this contraband anyway?"

Victoria hesitantly approached the portrait of the man questioning her and gestured to the recent hole in it. He studied it and Mrs. PIC did the same from over his shoulder. Finally, he muttered, "Illegal. Bullshit. Trash. Unpatriotic. Anti-American worker." Mrs. PIC nodded behind him.

After a brief silence, Mrs. PIC asked, "Where do you think she went?"

Mr. Walton-Clinton-Trump spent a long time thinking, then gestured for Victoria to leave the room, which she did. "We've caught her listening to enemy-sympathizer media before, but only when she was young. She might be hiding out in the palace, or she may have fled the country. We can call the council, or check security, or question the staff... But all of those would require making it known to some number of people that she's missing."

Mrs. Walton-Clinton-Trump sighed. "The council's never revealed our secrets before, nor have the staff. But if she doesn't return, we'll need a cover story. Who can we trust abiding by a cover story?"

"No one," Mr. Walton-Clinton-Trump replied immediately. "Anyone put in that position could use it to advance their own position. But, if only one or two or three people hear about it, no one will believe them. We can call them fanatics, lunatics, communists, heretics."

"Victoria's already heard," Mrs. Walton-Clinton-Trump said wisely. "So that leaves us with two people tops."

"Victoria is new and controversial. If she says anything, we can blame the gentlemen who ran the job fair."

"And women," Mrs. PIC added.

"We're not on camera," he reminded her. "But still, keeping to no more than two people would be wise. We'll discuss this with one of the council members, and from there we'll decide who else, if anyone, to include."

"I recommend the Head of Big Fashion, she's very loyal and marvelously knowledgeable in the latest trends. And she'd have the best insight into spotting Princess. She's been very much involved in her wardrobe. And of course, her knowledge is great in matters of Voguelle. She may have some huge input as far as that situation goes."

"I made the greatest decision, marrying you," Mr. PIC said (although the marriage had been mostly constructed by the parents of both parties, based largely on political power). "We'll consult with Big Fashion immediately in… your private office. She'll likely feel more at home there, with its womanly attributes."

They walked out the door together and instructed Victoria to enter the bedroom and remain there until they, or someone in their service, asked her to leave. She entered obediently and, upon the door closing and locking behind her (from the outside), began to shake with enthusiasm. "I'll be rich!" she muttered to herself, pacing around the room unsure of where and if she could sit.

The People In Charge walked with purpose to Mrs. Walton-Clinton-Trump's office where they called the Big Head of Fashion's personal cellphone.

"Mrs. Person In Charge!" she answered after just two rings, which was a bit more than she'd hoped, but she was out shopping in the field and not expecting a call. "Can I help you, ma'am? Looking for more juicy details on Voguelle, perhaps?" She'd saved a few minor things in case such an occasion were to arise.

"I require your presence in my private office immediately."

"I'm out on the field at the moment, but I'll be

returning immediately, of course. Twenty minutes perhaps and I'll be there. If you might inform security of my arrival, it may be faster."

"Make it faster," Mrs. PIC said. "And of course I'll let security know." She hung up as Mr. PIC was already dialing the Big Head of House Defense.

"The Head of Big Fashion will be arriving shortly. Assure that her passage is swift," he said after a few seconds. Having very little else to do, the Big Head of House Defense always answered the phone swiftly. Mr. PIC hung up, obviously having been given the correct response.

"Our daughter is out in the world, letting herself be seen in that... undesirable situation she's in." Mrs. PIC sighed.

"It's nothing a good technomancer can't deal with," Mr. PIC assured her. "We live in a great country. The greatest country with the greatest people working for us. This will be fine."

"Of course we do," Mrs. PIC said. "But don't forget, we're not on camera."

Precisely thirteen minutes later, The Head of Big Fashion knocked hastily on Mrs. PIC's door. Seconds later, the couple were dressed and had invited her to enter. They described their predicament to her, at first leaving out the vile propaganda Princess had left behind (which consisted mostly of records as she'd brought nearly the entirety of her tape and CD collection with her).

Ms. Big Head made herself appear thoughtful for a few moments, then suggested, "Perhaps it's simply an outburst of hormones. A sudden act of reb- of juvenile delinquency. The right pills could certainly fix that."

Mr. and Mrs. PIC looked at each other, then Mr. PIC said, "It wasn't so… sudden. We found a certain amount of illegal recordings in her room. Of propaganda."

"Ahhh," Ms. Big Head said and stared down at the floor, which is always the first step in putting matters delicately. "Then you believe she may have left in search of the source of said propaganda? Brainwashed perhaps." She paused and then added tentatively, "And you'd like to keep this quiet?"

"Yes," they said in unison. Mr. PIC continued, "You always express my thoughts so well. We don't plan on sharing this with more than one other person. Victoria, the new housekeeper, already knows, but we're certain she'll stay quiet. Unfortunately, I'm not sure it would be wise to share this information with Household Security, although they could possibly help us find her. Then there's also the matter of Voguelle."

"Ahhh," Ms. Big Head said again. She adjusted her shoulder pads, which were just small enough so that she could fit through the door. "It wouldn't be difficult to claim that she's on vacation, although this would certainly anger Voguelle. He may not be nearly as powerful as yourselves, but he's certainly a valuable asset. In fact, he'd be highly skilled at creating a potion to cure Miss Walton-Clinton-Trump of her… hormonal ills, were she here presently. So on one hand, I might suggest he be the other individual you inform. On the other hand, he has quite the reputation of political and capitalistic abilities as well."

"He sounds like a great man. Strong. I look forward to meeting him," Mr. PIC said.

"We'll have dinner with him first, not mention a

word about Princess, and read him like a book in the process," Mrs. PIC said.

"Brilliant," Mr. PIC said. "My brilliant wife. How smart I am to have married her."

Ms. Big Head's eyes flashed with opportunity. "In that case, may I offer my services in personally designing your attire for the night? Since the meeting has changed a bit, it seems to require a change of wardrobe as well. Something to emphasize your own remarkable strength and also your caring, fatherly side would be well fitting. As for you, Mrs. Walton-Clinton-Trump, I believe something that emphasizes your womanly wisdom would be quite advantageous."

"Very wise," Mr. PIC agreed. "You can accomplish this is an hour?"

"Certainly, I know your wardrobes very well. Might I also provide my humble input on dining arrangements?"

"Your input is always welcome," Mrs. PIC said.

"Since it will only be the three of you, I would suggest seating more intimate than a long table. It may be particularly advantageous if you sat at a more casual four-person table. I would even suggest Mr. Walton-Clinton-Trump seating himself across from The Grand Mage while Mrs. Walton-Clinton-Trump seats herself next to her husband."

"My dear," Mr. PIC said, suddenly turning to his wife. "I've just had the most brilliant idea." Upon hearing Mr. PIC's desire to adjust the seating arrangements, Mrs. PIC promptly sent Ms. Big Head off to inform the caterers.

Half an hour later, Mrs. PIC received a text that her ensemble was assembled. Upon arriving, she laid her eyes on the most beautiful dress she'd ever seen. It was even more beautiful once she put it on, or so Ms. Big Head informed her. Pale pink, it was cinched at the waist, modestly cut only halfway down the cleft of her breasts, and ended midthigh in the manner of a business dress. A light mesh was all that covered most of her back.

"Gorgeous," Mrs. PIC said.

"Bigly," Ms. Big Head said. "I'll leave you with your makeup specialist now. I need to assemble your husband's attire." And she swept herself out of the room like a hot summer wind just before a storm.

Mr. PIC was managing his social media when he received a private message from Ms. Big Head informing him that his dinner wear was ready. He checked the time. She was precisely two minutes early. He arrived at his chambers to find a black suit, with a rather large jacket including rather large shoulder pads, under which hung a light blue dress shirt and red tie. The gold buttons of the jacket were engraved with the donkephant, while the gold cufflinks held rather large diamonds. Under the hanger that Ms. Big Head held were a pair of subtly pumped up kicks (though the heels were quite high) in which sat a pair of tall, thin black socks. The uneducated would have called them stockings.

"Very good, Liberty. Very good," he said upon seeing it. Ms. Big Head blushed. It was rare the President called anyone by name.

"Thank you, Mr. Person In Charge," she said. "I'll leave you to dress then?"

He nodded and began to undress as she left the room. Although she recognized the opportunity for advancement, she also recognized that Mrs. PIC, although not particularly intelligent, was the smarter of the two and did not want to risk a liaison.

At precisely two after eight, Mrs. PIC entered the dining hall and sat at the small table, diagonal from Voguelle. He was wearing baggy black slacks which gathered around his ankles (making his light blue socks quite visible) with a tight black dress shirt, the sleeves of which widened around his elbows, but gathered well before his wrists. Only the bottom three buttons were buttoned. Over this he wore a long flowing black cape. Mrs. PIC could immediately sense his magical abilities by the way his cape continued to flow even while he sat in a breezeless room. A number of plastic plants had been set in the room to make it feel a bit less empty, the long table having been removed. There was also a banner advertising The America on the wall to Mrs. PIC's left. Mrs. PIC extended her right hand. "A pleasure to meet you, Voguelle," she said, with emphasis on his name.

"A great pleasure, Mrs. Walton-Clinton-Trump In Charge," the Grand Mage replied, with emphasis on 'great.'

"I hope your journey wasn't too difficult?" she asked.

"No, no bother," he said. "A few blocks beyond my usual vicinity, but I'm always willing to make time for a worthy cause." The Grand Mage sipped on his glass of water until a caterer appeared carrying four bottles of wine, at which point The Grand Mage chose a glass of dry white wine, while Mrs. PIC chose a glass of sweet red. Him being a man and her being a woman, she knew this was quite acceptable, although she'd have to subtly suggest to her husband to a chose a dry white or perhaps something manlier.

"So, Mr. Voguelle," Mrs. PIC said, "Tell me about your experience." She tuned him out just seconds after he began to speak and minutes later Mr. PIC entered the room and sat across from Voguelle. She wasn't sure and didn't care whether she was interrupting when she said, "Mr. Voguelle, this is my husband, Mr. Walton-Clinton-Trump In Charge."

Mr. PIC waited for Voguelle to extend his hand, then gripped it and tried his best to pull Voguelle out of his seat and towards him. Strength was always important when meeting strong people. The mage countered with a spell of immobility, leaving his arm yanked forward but his ass firmly planted in its cushioned seat.

"A pleasure, Mr. Person In Charge," said Voguelle.

"Indeed. I'm sure you've enjoyed speaking with my beautiful wife. Let's get down to business now, I'm sure you've worked up an appetite on your way here." Mr. PIC clapped his hands and a short woman in a tiny black dress scurried out from the kitchen carrying a golden platter of French fries and hot dog spears with sides of ketchup, nacho cheese, and Dijon mustard. Mr. PIC grinned merrily. "Appetizers," he said to Voguelle.

After everyone had something on their plate, Mr. PIC began, amidst mouthfuls of food, "So Voguelle, may I call you Voguelle? Voguelle, there's been some unfortunate circumstances recently." He swallowed a slurry of fries and hot dog. "And you won't be able to meet with Princess today."

"Oh?" Voguelle said. "I hope she's well."

"So do we," Mrs. PIC muttered, glancing around to assure no servers were eavesdropping.

"Oh?" said Voguelle, with genuine curiosity.

"She… left earlier today. It would have been rude to cancel our meeting with such short notice. But I trust you won't inform anyone of this embarrassment."

"You're placing quite a political strain on me, Mr. Walton-Clinton-Trump. My reputation is at risk here. A small number of very wealthy individuals know of our arrangement and if they don't see my success, they'll assume I've failed."

"We'll make sure to speak highly of you, Voguelle," Mrs. PIC said. "The people know that we don't just throw praise around haphazardly."

"Thank you, Mrs. Walton-Clinton-Trump. I should also add that your dress is lovely and your husband's suit is rather spectacular as well."

They spent some time exchanging praises and after a few moments, Mr. PIC clapped for the main course to arrive. The short woman in the black dress scurried back out and placed a golden plate in front of each of them. Each plate held two burgers on, what tasted to Voguelle like Kaiser rolls, with the crust removed. One burger featured cheddar cheese, a mound of bacon, and Thousand Island. A toothpick was pierced through it, holding on a sprig of cilantro. Upon taking a bite, Voguelle could clearly taste that it had been fried in wine. The second burger included mozzarella sticks, stewed tomatoes, and a bit of coleslaw.

Voguelle and the PIC resumed praising each other when the server left, and as they ate, Voguelle even brought out a few party tricks. He waved his hand about and muttered a few words, and in the center of the table there appeared a marvelous pair of sneakers. The sides of each read in gold blocky print "Walton-Clinton-

Trump." The left was blue and the right was red and diamonds were set in along the soles. Obviously having dazzled the couple, after beginning his second burger, he waved his hand over the sneakers and whispered a few more words and the sneakers grew heels. Just when they appeared to have stopped changing, the wedges turned into stilettos.

Mr. PIC found this so marvelous that after desert arrived (deep-fried donuts smothered in ice cream), he said to Voguelle, "You are obviously a highly skilled magician of fashion. So highly skilled that I may offer you a position here at the Gold House." Mrs. PIC nodded her head encouragingly.

Voguelle feigned modesty at first, then finally said, "It's truly an honor, Mr. PIC, but I fear threatening the Head of Big Fashion's position. She's quite a charming woman with a good head on her elegant shoulders. I must decline, with much disappointment."

"There must b something we can do," Mrs. PIC texted Mr. PIC under the table.

Mr. PIC looked up from his phone and said to Voguelle, "What position might you consider, Voguelle? Any you like."

Voguelle again feigned modesty. He brushed a hand through his luscious locks and even managed to blush a bit. "There is one that might benefit all of us," he began. "It seems that, Princess having departed so quickly, that you're left without an heir. You're left with no one to run against the other candidates once you grow tired of the difficult work of managing the state." He paused here to let the implications sink in and judge the couple's reactions. When he saw that nothing appeared to register, he continued, "Perhaps I might be honored with such a position. Your new heir. That is, until Princess returns, if you wish." Mr. Walton-Clinton-Trump opened his mouth to say something, but Voguelle quickly added, "I'm sure you will find my loyalty and secret-keeping abilities quite worthy, if perhaps not my other more magical abilities."

"I like you, Voguelle," Mr. PIC said. "You're a strong man. So strong, you're like my son if I had one. Eating dinner with you today gave me a brilliant idea." Voguelle raised his eyebrows and hid a smirk as Mr. PIC continued, "How'd you like to be my heir?"

$$$

Princess awoke as if she had just slipped into a nightmare. She'd had the most beautiful dream of a never-ending concert in a land without cameras on every street corner, in a land with no real streets, where people wore what they felt like wearing and no one counted her calories. And a man, she couldn't remember his name—Evil Baby?—had given her fried dough covered in powdered sugar and she'd even tasted beer, real beer. She rolled over in her bed, which felt much less fluffy than usual, and realized she still tasted beer.

Princess opened her eyes to find herself lying on a pile of blankets in a small red and white striped tent. Sunlight shone in through the fabric. There was a bucket sitting on the ground next to her blankets and her new boots sat at the other end. She sat up and began to laugh, genuinely laugh, not like she did at the politicians' jokes or when the laugh tracks played on television. It was a strange sound, like a woman crying with occasional chimpanzee-like panting. When she'd finally stopped, she noticed a sticky note on the bucket. It read in exquisitely tiny red ink:

Princess,

Didn't realize you were such a lightweight. Hope you still remember how to find your way around the Stage. You're just outside the back entrance. When you're feeling up for it, go back in and find Occasum at Sick Sustenance. Just left of the entrance, can't miss it. Bet they can fix you up.

—Stanislaus

She stood up and looked around the room, and finding nothing important besides her boots, put them on. Then she spotted her purse in the corner. She rushed over to it, picked it up, and hugged it. Then she headed out. Outside the tent, the sun was incredibly bright. She returned her sunglasses and hat to her head. A young woman sat on a bench amidst dozens of tents similar to the one Princess had just left. A small stereo, with smaller versions of the mirrors and battery that were on Sandworm's vehicle, quietly played Spanish guitar. Occasionally a chorus would shout, "Muertos!" (although Princess had no idea that was a word) and some quiet reedy instrument would play an arpeggio. The woman was clearly absorbed in a book she was holding, but when she caught Princess's movement out of the corner of her eye, she smiled and gave her a nod. Princess returned the gesture and headed for The Stage's back door.

Upon reaching it, she realized she had no idea what to do, so after trying the handle, she knocked three times as she'd seen Sandworm and Occasum do. "Aye!" a gravelly voice shouted from somewhere inside.

"Hi!" Princess shouted. "I'm Princess Walton-Clinton-Trump. I was here last night. I actually have this note from Stanislaus telling me to go back to The Stage."

"I know who you are!" the voice shouted back. The door made no appearance of opening. "What was your favorite song last night?"

"I... don't know. Stanislaus's band was really good, but whoever was on before them, they might be my favorite."

"Didn't answer my question."

"The song they were playing when I got here. It had to be four or five songs before their last one. That was my favorite."

The door opened and an elderly man, covered in tattoos and wearing only overalls, appeared. "Wouldn't normally let someone in that easy, but since you're comin' from the hangover camp and you're new and all. Band was Swamp Slut. Probably Keep Diggin' or Deer Bones is the one you're thinkin' of."

"Thanks," Princess said, repeating the titles to herself as she walked through the small foyer. It was much smaller than the foyer at the main entrance, although there was still a small merch table set up. She scoured it for Swamp Slut, and finding none, realized her money was probably no good here anyway. When she exited the foyer, she turned to her left and immediately saw a gargoyle holding a wooden sign in its talons that read, "Sick Sustenance." Intermittently, green goo spewed from the gargoyle's mouth and into a large bucket below. In the short trip to the establishment, part of which was built into the outer wall of the arena and part of which consisted of a long wooden pavilion, Princess saw a number of people grab a cup from a stand next to the bucket and scoop up some of the green goo.

Occasum appeared at her side just as Princess was sniffing the bucket. It smelled minty and a little sweet and also a little like lawn trimmings. "Go ahead and grab some," Occasum said, causing Princess to jump.

"I don't have any way to pay for it," Princess said, suddenly feeling poor. She fought back tears for a moment.

"This shit's up for grabs," Occasum said. "No one pays for it. Purely public service. Bet it'll make your head and your stomach feel better too."

Princess looked at the thermos Marion had given her, and finding the water gone, opened it and scooped some of the green goo up as she'd seen other people do. Then she asked, "What's wrong with my head and stomach?" For a moment, she thought this might be the miracle cure for her weight problem.

"You're not hungover?" Occasum asked. "Nauseous? Headache?" Princess shook her head and took a sip of the green stuff. It tasted just like it smelled but was also delightfully cold. She smiled at Occasum, who was staring at her in confusion. A little girl with blue pigtails skipped over and grabbed herself some goo. She waved at them, then skipped away, slurping. Finally, Occasum said, "You seemed pretty drunk. At least we know you've got one skill. I don't suppose you know anything about cooking or herbs or…"

Princess looked even more dumbfounded. "I know how to tell parsley from cilantro," she said. "The soup spoon is the rounder one. The seafood fork is the tiniest."

Occasum nodded slowly. "Follow me." She headed

towards the section of Sick Sustenance that was built into the wall. They passed a counter with a long line of customers leading up to it, then entered a hallway with one door leading to the area behind the counter and two doors past that, one on the right and one on the left.

"Where're we going?" Princess asked. They entered the room on the left, which smelled distinctly of eucalyptus.

"Found a job for you," Occasum said.

The room was full of sinks. Four sinks to be precise. In front of one stood a burly man with a handlebar mustache and a heart with an arrow through it tattooed on his cheek. In front of the other stood a teenage girl with a ponytail that almost reached the backs of her knees. Both wore t-shirts and shorts with bleach stains. On the far wall was a rack containing clean plates, cups, bowls, silverware, and a smattering of cookware that Princess didn't have names for.

"I, um, it's my first day here," Princess said.

"Yeah. You work here, you earn your own food and your own room for the second day." Occasum looked Princess up and down. "Actually, you even got yourself a second outfit. I doubt you wanna get your new clothes all grubby." Occasum held the door open. "Come on, I'll give you some clothes you won't mind staining. You can change back into that when you're done working." Princess followed her back into the hallway. "We usually work six-hour shifts here. After you get the hang of things, you can adjust that if you want." They opened the door that had been on Princess's right with a key they pulled out of their hair to reveal a tiny room with a stairway, two folding chairs, and a mirror on the wall. Occasum locked the door behind them. They replaced the key into their liberty spike. "Wait here," Occasum said, then jogged up the stairs.

Princess sat down and pouted. Everything had seemed so promising last night. Now they were trying to get her to wash dishes. Occasum came running back down the stairs and held out a bleach-stained black tank top and a pair of torn jeans. "These should fit," they said, looking her up and down. "Maybe a little baggy, but I think they'll stay up at least." Princess tentatively grabbed them with her thumb and pointer finger. "You can change here if you want, I'll turn around. I mean, I could also take you upstairs and show you the room you can have if you want it, but I think you'd like it better if you let me clean it up before you see it." They chuckled.

Princess sighed. "I'll change here. I mean, there's a mirror." And she thought, "If I'm already going to wear this disgusting outfit, I might as well go all the way. What's the worst that could happen?" She undressed and dressed quickly and checked herself out in the mirror. And gasped. The bleach stains on her tank top were so perfectly placed, it looked like something the Big Head of Fashion might have designed. The holes her jeans were equally well placed and their baggy boyfriend fit tied the whole thing together. "This is so bum chic!" Princess squealed.

"Does that mean you're dressed?" Occasum asked.

"Yeah," Princess said. "Are you sure it's okay for me to keep these? Who designed them?"

Occasum laughed harder and turned around. "Dishwashing and various other jobs designed them. But yeah, as long as you're working here for at least a few days, they're yours. Getting a little tight on me anyway. By the way, we could use your help, so I hope you stay here, but if you really hate it, you can always ask around and see who else could use some help."

"Thank you!" Princess said. She imagined herself sitting behind a desk somewhere, nodding and smiling at people, and decided she'd ask around later.

Occasum walked her back to the sink room. "I leave you here. I'll be on the other side of that counter if you need me." They gestured to the small counter where some sunlight shone through and a lot of heat drifted from the ovens. "This here is Ramblin' Cat." They gestured to the burly man with the face tattoo. He turned around and nodded to her, a broad toothy smile across his face. "And this is Alejandra Cierraczak."

The girl with the incredibly long hair raised a soapy hand and waved without turning around. "Looking forward to working with you," she said. Princess could tell from her lessons on using a phone voice that the girl was smiling.

"If you need any help, these two are the people to ask. They got this down to an art," Occasum said and left the room.

"Nice to meet you," Princess said warily. "So, um, where do I start?"

Ramblin' Cat gestured to the two unoccupied sinks. "Pick a favorite," he said. "And then grab some dishes." He gestured to a wheeled cart standing between himself and the girl.

Princess approached the cart and tentatively picked up a plate. "Um, I think there's been a mistake here. There's some sort of brown sauce on this plate." Her coworkers laughed and it made her uneasy.

"That's why we're washing them," Ramblin' Cat said so gently that her intelligence wasn't insulted.

"Oh," said Princess and took the plate over to a sink catty-cornered from him. She set it down like someone who never wants kids sets down a baby with a dirty diaper, then she slowly turned a faucet and watched the water pour over it.

"Easier when you put a bunch in the sink at once," Alejandra said without turning away from her sink.

"Thanks." Princess grabbed a few more plates and a couple of bowls and set them all down. "So, how do I know when they're clean?"

Ramblin' Cat set a huge pile of dishes, Princess wasn't sure how he could carry them all at once, on the shelves. Then walked over to Princess's sink. He said, "So the next thing you want to do is add soap." He pointed at a bottle of soap sitting opposite them. "Then you want to grab this." He picked up a dishcloth that had been sitting neatly folded next to the sink. A vomiting skull was printed on it. "You scrub the dishes with it until they've all been soaped and all of them look spotless. If you still aren't sure, smell 'em. If you aren't sure after that, ask me or Ala." Princess picked up the bottle of soap and squirted it all over the sink, then began to scrub the dishes. "You don't need quite that much soap," Ramblin' Cat added, returning to his own sink. "Next time, try like a quarter of that amount."

Princess realized the soap was where the eucalyptus smell had been coming from. She also realized that if she pretended she was only touching the soap, dishwashing wasn't so bad. Once she finished washing, she picked them each up individually and examined them for food. Alejandra was bringing her third pile of dishes over since Princess began washing and she paused to watch Princess. After having examined every dish with her eyes, Princess picked up the last dish and smelled it. Then she turned around and jumped to see Alejandra watching her. "I think they're good?" Princess asked, staring into Alejandra's brown almond eyes. They were especially accentuated with heavy eyeliner drawn out into wings and green eyeshadow the color of pine trees powdered up to her eyebrows. Black lipstick marred her lips, but Princess had almost begun to get used to that.

Alejandra inspected the dishes. "Perfect," she said. "Now you just need to get a little faster." She left Princess to carry them over to the shelves by herself, which took her two trips. When she returned to the cart to grab more, she found it empty. Without turning around, Alejandra said, "There should be more at the window."

Princess turned around and found a great number of stacks there. Just as delicately as she had set that first plate down, she placed the piles on the cart and wheeled it back. The next five hours continued similarly, although Princess did eventually pick up enough speed that she washed only half as quickly as her co-workers. Although she didn't pick up on it, her co-workers also began to accept her. Slowly, but surely, they began to banter and bitch in her presence.

When Occasum opened the door, Alejandra was saying, "You see how much stewed tomato is still on this plate? I could feed a family of mice for a day on this! What are the bussers doing?"

Occasum laughed. "The mouse population is doing

fine," they said. "Tomatoes would be better as compost, but they're so acidic…"

"We should get more bins then," Alejandra said, suddenly becoming serious. "Gotta be something they'd be good for."

"Good idea," said Occasum. "I'll see if I can find any. I'm heading out now though. Princess, you got your six hours in. You're welcome to go enjoy the show, get some food from this place, wander around. I don't know what you're into." They walked out into the hallway together.

"Whose playing?" Princess asked.

"The Laughing Rats, right now." Then remembering that Princess wasn't familiar with these newer bands, they added, "They have a pirate ska thing going on. A lot of upbeats. Trumpet and bagpipes. Actually, you should probably go check them out. They might fill in the gaps between the shit you were listening to and the shit you'll be hearing here."

Princess nodded, then remembered that she was still in her work clothes. "Should I change first?"

"Up to you. Might be a good idea since you only have like three outfits." They caught Princess's mortified facial expression and added, "I'm sure you'll get more soon, if you keep working like you did today." Princess nodded and followed Occasum to the stairwell. They brought her clothes down and she changed while Occasum worked on the room upstairs. They'd instructed her to leave her work clothes under the first stair, and following instructions, Princess realized that there was a shelf under each stair. She tucked the clothes away and left the inner part of the restaurant.

The food smelled even better in the hallway and once Princess went outside, her stomach was growling. There was a line of five people to the counter and after some deliberation, she got in line and stared up at the menu. Veggie burgers, kombucha, seasonal fruit salad, seasonal veggie salad, an assortment of teas, chef's soup, scrambled eggs with a wide array of add-ons, toast with an even wider selection of add-ons. By the time it was Princess's turn to order she was salivating but still had no idea what she wanted and still didn't know what a number of the menu items even were. "Chicken tacos," she decided at random.

"Any specific toppings?" the man at the counter asked. Seeing her confusion, he added, "Our usual is lettuce, tomato, sour cream, refried beans, mixed cheese."

Out of calorie-counting habit, Princess said, "No sour cream." The man nodded and walked towards the back of the kitchen. Princess stood where she'd seen the other customers waiting for food. Ten or so minutes later, another man brought Princess's meal to the counter where she stood. Realizing she hadn't paid anything, she stuttered, "I, um, Occasum said I could…"

"You work here, it's cool dude. Eat whatever, eat whenever," he said, and handed her a plate of delightfully steaming tacos.

She wandered over to one of the long picnic tables under the tent, specifically where there was no one nearby, and sat down. She couldn't remember ever eating a meal this big. After two tacos, she found herself too full to cram anymore in. She watched the other customers, looking to see where they brought their plates to and discovered a second, smaller counter near where she'd ordered. However, when Princess set her plate on the counter, the woman who'd been taking everyone else's dishes frowned out her. "What's wrong with it?" she asked, staring down at the plate.

"It was delicious," Princess said. "Just can't eat anymore."

"Where're you from?" she asked, taking another customer's plate and setting it on a cart similar to the one Princess had been taking dirty dishes from.

"The America," Princess said.

"Ahh," said the woman. "Ms. Walton-Clinton-Trump. No hard feeling this time, but around here, we only order what we can eat. Or share. Next time might want to half your order. Today though, I'll take care of these." The woman popped one of the tacos into her mouth - the whole taco—and managed to dismiss Princess with an inclination of her head toward the inner portion of the Stage.

Princess wandered out of the pavilion and into the crowd and bobbed around. The music did sound like ska to her, although a far cry from The Specials or any of the other bands she'd discovered while in The America. The lead singer was a tall, lanky and badly sunburned man wearing a white sunbonnet and otherwise dressed entirely in military-style camo gear. Sweat poured down his face as he screamed into the microphone. Something about perturbation, masturbation, sweat flies, and cold eyes. Once in a while, he'd jump a bit and do something weird with his feet. The people closer to the stage were doing the same thing while violently swinging their arms in a jogging motion. Some were even headbanging at the same time. Princess wondered how they kept their balance. As she watched, she recognized Stanislaus in the crowd. He spotted her and danced through the crowd over to where she was bobbing.

"Wanna learn how to jig?" he shouted over a particularly (and purposefully) out of tune bagpipe solo.

Princess cringed. "Maybe later. I'm not really feeling this."

He nodded, or maybe just headbanged. "You work with Occasum today?"

"Yeah. It was… different."

"Good," he shouted. "You can always go socialize over there. Or grab yourself a drink and head outside the Stage. Usually people milling around waiting for their jams to play or looking to trade and whatever. Love this band though! I'll be here."

The bagpipes squealed again and Princess nodded, turning back towards Sick Sustenance. She picked up a big paper cup and scooped out some goo from the bucket before turning to the passage she'd used to enter the arena seven or so hours ago. She didn't recognize anyone and no one recognized her and she thought this was thrilling. Not too far past the hangover tent, a circle of people sitting on blankets was starting to form. She walked casually by, sipping her goop and doing her best to look uninterested. Near the center of the circle, or what Princess imagined would become the center once the circle fully formed, were three orbs, each about the size of her head, that began to flicker now and again.

Princess had only seen strange circles like this from the Head of Big Necromancy and some of his sorcerous friends, and then it had almost always been to summon more voters for the polls. Her curiosity got the best of her and she approached the crowd. That's when she spotted Ramblin' Cat, only he was mostly covered in corpse paint. His face tattoo appeared to have been stenciled in over the paint.

"Hey, what's up newb?" he asked. A woman sitting on a blanket next to him, also in corpse paint, and a man sitting on the same blanket whose face appeared to be tie-dyed turned around and watched her.

"Just, uh, just walking around. You holding some kind of ritual here?" she said.

All three of them laughed. "You could say that," said Ramblin' Cat. He caught her looking suspiciously at the orbs. "Oh those. Those are just solar lights. Way better for the environment than bonfires. And no waste. Rose here helped design them." He gestured to the woman and she waved. Ramblin' Cat lowered his voice, "She's brilliant, but she'll never admit it. Should be teaching science."

"I heard that!" the woman said. "You know I've had a couple apprentices in my days. I'm not hoarding all the physics to myself."

Ramblin' Cat turned around and faced the other two for a moment and when they both nodded, he turned back around to face Princess, "You're welcome to join us if you want."

Princess was about to instinctively say no, but realizing she had absolutely nothing else to do, she joined the circle and shook their hands. "So what're you doing out here?" she asked.

"Enjoying the evening," said Rose. Then she added, "Actually, since we got a newb here, it might be a good night for ghost stories once it's dark."

A few people in the larger group shouted things like, "Hell yeah!" In the meantime, Princess learned all about solar power, which at first she found incredibly boring, but became interested in once the solar orbs began to emit steadier light. She realized the lights in the arena were doing the same thing, even the glowing signs. Upon very confidently pointing this out, she discovered that some of these things were actually wind-powered. In addition, there were other similar buildings that used hydro-power.

By the time Ramblin' Cat stood up and bellowed, "Raiding Party!" Princess had developed a headache from taking in so much new information. Then a mob of people wearing sparkling bellbottoms and flouncy shirts, some with large medallions around their necks, came rushing out of the bushes with brightly colored guns.

"Colors will run tonight!" a woman at the front the mob screamed and pulled the trigger on her assault styled rifle. Princess screamed. The portion of the circle closest to the woman was immediately soaked in water. They stood up, gripping their blankets and towels. Some held them up as shields, while many of the towels were used to whip at the mob. After most of the party was soaked and the water guns apparently empty, the mob retreated back into the bushes.

"What was that?" Princess yelled, hiding behind Ramblin' Cat, along with the man who'd been sharing the blanket with Rose.

"Damn Discotech," Ramblin' Cat growled. Rose spread the blanket back out on the ground. Some of her corpse paint was dripping down onto her t-shirt. When they all sat down, Princess could see that Ramblin' Cat's was as well. Some of the party had completely lost their face paint. There were chuckles and curses all around.

"One day," someone said from the other side of the circle. "We're gonna creep up on that Discotech and paint the whole thing black."

"Your great-grandmomma used to say that too," someone countered. "Never happens though."

Rose clapped her hands. "It appears to be quite dark now," she said. There was silence for a few moments, then she began. "A long time ago, many hundreds of years have passed since, a small settlement formed atop a swamp." Princess's ears perked up, but she didn't dare interrupt to ask what a swamp was. "They built tents and then huts atop the small bars of solid land between the squishy soil and the pools and creeks. They found food in the swamp. Bark and nuts and berries. Water filtered by the numerous plants.

"But as they grew, they found their supplies grew less and less. The more they chopped down trees, the fewer nuts they found, and the more nuts they ate, the fewer trees grew. The more they shit in the water, the more the water began to make them sick. The swamp seemed to torture them, and out of spite, they made a pact to survive and grow and procreate. As the town grew into a city, women and children began to disappear, but the people created laws and technology to solve these problems. They kept the women and children inside. They made machines to find fresh water. They found new things to burn for light and fuel.

"Until one day, they no longer needed the swamp. A brave man, seeking to reassure the people, seeking to be a good leader, called all the people together. He stood on a podium and shouted out at what remained of the swamp. 'You can't hurt us now, devil!,' he cried. 'We have conquered thee! And we do not fear thee!' I can't be sure how much time passed, but the man continued to lead the people and the swamp continued to whimper beneath their rulership. Until one day, the swamp gave up, and when the swamp gave up, it collapsed in on itself. The city fell into the holes of empty aquifers and coal mines. Slowly but surely, the swamp began to gather itself back together. Trees and bushes began to grow again." A number of people glanced warily at the bushes where the mob has sprung from. "But the people, having sworn to defeat the swamp, bide their time down in the mines. And one day, they might just reach up from the ground and... GRAB YOU!" Rose grabbed Princess's foot and chuckled as she jumped up.

"Classic slasher horror!" someone cheered from the circle.

A cool wind blew from the east, rustling the blankets and the bushes and trees. Princess wondered what everyone found in such a strange story. But a moment later, another speaker began to tell their own tale, and Princess became lost in the love of Dracula and Mina. The night went on like this until she found herself uncontrollably yawning and remembered that Occasum had prepared a room for her. She politely excused herself from the circle and wandered off back into the Stage. She was surprised to see that Sick Sustenance was still serving food and on a dreamlike whim, bought herself a veggie burger, which she carried up to her room along with her empty paper cup. Ramblin' Cat had told her to hang onto it when she threw it on the ground and she wasn't sure how long she was supposed to keep it. She walked into the hallway and found a note on the mirror, addressed to her, informing her that her room was up the stairs and third door on the right. It also said that if she had any questions, to press a buzzer at the fourth door on the left. It was signed by Occasum.

She followed the instructions and opened her door to find a twin bed, lifted off the floor by shelving. There was a nightstand next to it with a lamp sitting on it and an orb, similar to the ones Princess had seen minutes before outside the Stage, hanging from the ceiling (although it wasn't glowing). The room was illuminated by the crescent moon shining through a large window. When she walked over to the lamp and flipped the switch, she found a key sitting on the nightstand and another sticky note. This one informed her that the key was for the door. It also informed her that her clothes and purse were on the dresser, which she hadn't previously noticed. Then she noticed a poster on the wall next to the window. It showed Swamp Slut posing in front of, what Princess now assumed from Rose's story must be, a swamp. With overwhelming happiness, she sat down on the bed and devoured her burger. She found she actually felt better when she ate more. Then she laid down, sticking her earbuds in her ears, and fell asleep to an Agent Orange cassette.

Her days continued to be much like this one, although on the third day, her tape player and her MP3 player both ran out of battery life. Upon hearing this, Rose asked to borrow them for a couple days. She returned them with new, rechargeable batteries and a solar-powered battery charger. She was to leave this charger on her windowsill.

Another day, Princess heard Twisted Sister playing from a smaller arena just west of The Stage (by now she'd learned how to tell the cardinal directions). Ramblin' Cat asked her if she'd like to check out his favorite job, what he did for a living when he wasn't dishwashing. They walked over to this other arena, which was also made of adobe, but the adobe was covered in what looked like finger paintings. A sign at the entrance read, "The Playground." Inside, she found it really was a playground, with swings and slides and two basketball courts, but like The Stage, the outer wall was filled with rooms. In many of them, kids sat at desks, in some babies slept in cribs. Also like the Stage, there was an actual stage inside, at the moment there were ten teenagers up there rocking out. On top of one section of the strange school was a telescope. And there was also a beautiful garden, as lush at Marion's had been, although this one was genuinely outside, in real sunlight. "Do you... make swings sets?" Princess asked tentatively. He laughed and shook his head. He taught first grade, usually in the evenings for the kids who were night owls.

After a few months, Princess began trying her hand at a few other jobs. She wasn't a fan of composting, due mostly to the smell, magnified by the summer heat. Janitorial work was a bit too unpredictable for her, although it was much cooler. But she managed to work as a gardener for five days by the time autumn rolled around. She found that the people here had small gardens placed all over the place, some hidden in lightly forested areas, others placed close to the structures where the sun would hit them for many hours. She was introduced to crop rotation and companion planting (and found both very superstitious but listened attentively nonetheless). Unfortunately, she soon found she simply could not remember the names of all the various plants.

However, it was while gardening that Princess became incredibly curious about the other communities in New Mexico, besides the Stage. Just across a small forest where she had been picking apples and dill, she saw a large, diamond-shaped structure glittering in the afternoon sun. When she listened carefully, she could hear deep base rhythms and fast, rhythmic vocals (although she couldn't make out any words) drifting from the building. After she'd filled up both her baskets and brought them back to Donna (who spent most of their time together, when not explaining how food grows, asking questions about Thelemita), she searched through the crowd at the show for Stanislaus. At first, she tried jumping up and down and waving to get his attention, but he started copying her, assuming it was her new dance move. Finally she hopped and waved her way over to him.

"Hey Stanislaus!" she screamed over the onslaught of blast beats. "What's that shiny glass thing to the east of here?"

"Nother community!" he yelled back. "Into rap over there!"

"Can I visit? Are they friendly?" she asked.

"Didn't know you were into rap!" he said. She made a 'hmph' noise and he shouted, "I'm not your parent!

Go if you want! They're just people, like us!"

Princess nodded and danced her way back out of the crowd. The sun was still up and she wanted to find out what rap was. Princess changed into her black boots, a recently acquired long black skirt with pockets, and her white corset, then marched off into the woods. The leaves crunched under her feet and she made a conscious effort not to step on any mushrooms hiding under them, sticking to the path as much as she could see it. By the time she emerged on the other side of the trees, her eyes having adjusted to the evening shadows, the setting sun's reflection on the building was nearly blinding. She put on her sunglasses, which she had begun to carry everywhere, and made a beeline for the diamond.

Upon closer inspection, she realized the diamond was actually attached to a low, ring-shaped wall, but not quite low enough for her to see over. The mirrors, as she'd expected, appeared to be solar panels. What she didn't expect was a slow chanting hidden under the bass of the music or the vibrations from said bass pulsing through her feet. She couldn't understand most of the lyrics because the singer was so fast (or any of the chanting, which she assumed was gibberish), but once in a while she heard "bitch" or "dick" or "spaghetti." She spent a long time wandering around until she caught sight of a big man in a spotless black suit walking with a big man in gym shorts and high-topped sneakers. There was something exceedingly cool about the way they walked.

She turned around and walked towards them, subconsciously trying to imitate their swagger. "Hi!" she called.

They looked at each other and shook their heads. Then the man in the suit began to wave his hands around with some sort of rhythm while speaking just as quickly as the music that was playing. Up close she could see that he was bald, but his head was tattooed with the image of a unicorn and some emojis. She cupped her ear, trying to catch what he was saying.

Finally he stopped and asked in a normal voice, "Well you know that one or not?"

Princess shook her head, but realized she was probably being vetted the same way she'd been at the Stage. "I've never heard rap before," she said. "Just wanted to see if I like it, maybe meet some new people."

The men looked at each other again and the shirtless one said, "Well how're we supposed to know if you're a poser then?"

Princess shrugged. "I'd have to be some sort of loser to pose as someone that doesn't know anything about the music they're trying to hear."

The gentlemen nodded and gestured for her to follow them. They headed to a corner where the diamond and the ring met and asked her what her name was. Princess told them and they shook hands and introduced themselves as Big Kid and Awesome Mike. She followed them delightedly through a steel door and into a cozy room with a bar and a pool table. They all walked up to the bartender and, seeing Big Mike and Awesome Kid (or whatever their names were) sit down on the stools, Princess sat down. The bartender was a vivacious lady in a white tank with a big carnival ticket made of aluminum hanging from a chain around her neck.

"Aye, Spiffy," one of the guys said.

"What can I do you for, Awesome Mike?" Spiffy asked, eyeing Princess up and down.

"Got us a newb," Awesome Mike said.

"Whatcha got?" Spiffy asked Princess.

"Um." Princess fumbled around in her pockets and found a lighter. "This?" she asked.

"I mean, let me hear you freestyle," Spiffy said. "They tradin' with lighters over at the Stage now? We been usin' medallions."

Big Kid took over for Princess. "She's never heard rap before, so we all figure she can't be a poser. You think we should let her in?"

"You just want to hear the show?" Spiffy asked, eyebrows raised almost to the top of her forehead.

"I just came from there, yeah," Princess said. "I'm exploring. You know, branching out."

Spiffy shrugged and gestured to the door on the other side of the room and smiled and waved as Princess got up. She was surprised to see that they let her just wander in, no guards or anything.

When she opened the door, she was immediately blasted in the face with an airhorn. She wasn't unused to this. However, what she saw shocked her. People here were dancing. Really dancing. As in, not that differently from what Princess was used to seeing in The America. Some of them were getting low, some of them were grinding, some of them were twerking. She would've felt right at home if the music wasn't so foreign to her. Not only was the beat catchy, but the lyrics were too and the harder she listened, she realized they had meaning, unlike the repetition of brand names she was so used to. She spent an hour dancing nonstop, then wandered back to the door she'd entered through. It was fun, but her heart wasn't in it. She said her goodbyes to Spiffy, who was still behind the bar, and left.

Outside the door, she ran into Big Kid and Awesome Mike again. It was dark now and they were concerned that she'd have trouble making it back. In the end, one of them, she still couldn't remember who had which name, walked her to her side of the woods. "Come back anytime you like!" he hollered over his shoulder.

Princess had been in New Mexico for exactly a year when she got up the guts to ask Donna where she thought Thelemita was. It was twilight in the spring and the grass was exceptionally soft. They were both barefoot, wandering along the edge of the woods. Princess had asked if Donna would help her study plants a bit more, at least the poisonous ones. Donna, already lubricated with wine, began to sob loudly, and between sobs, got out the words, "Don't you know deported?" Princess shook her head and stormed her brain for some way to make this less awkward. She was still storming when Donna calmed herself down enough to say, "If she's not dead, she's a slave laborer." Princess gulped and her face reddened with anger and sadness and a bit of embarrassment.

Chapter 5
The Return

Princess banged on the door to Backstage. "Stanislaus Ramirez!" she hollered and began kicking the door with her steel-toed boots. Eyeliner was running down her cheeks.

When he opened the door, his usual grin (which was enhanced by a decent amount of liquor since it was 11 pm by now) quickly transformed into a concerned frown. "Are you okay?" he asked, spreading his arms in a way that invited a hug if she wanted one, but didn't put any pressure on her.

She stared him dead in the eye. "Deportation. I thought that meant getting sent here. Or getting sent back to wherever you came from."

Stanislaus shook his head. "You don't know what that wall's for?" he asked, gesturing vaguely to the north. "No one actually wants to go to The America, although it's rumored there was a time they were dying to. That wall is to keep people in."

Princess grimaced. "I have to go back," she said. "If I tell my parents. Or if I become President... I can fix this."

Stanislaus stood silent for a long time, chewing on his lip. "I can't help you with that one. I don't know what it's like there by now. If you really think you can change it, I'm all for it." He was trying to keep the admiration and the sadness both out of his voice.

"I'm packing tonight," Princess said. "I'll leave tomorrow morning."

"If you want," Stanislaus said. "I can arrange someone to drive you part way."

Princess nodded. "Rock on, dude." She hugged him and headed quickly to her room. There, she sat her many-pocketed shorts, bleach-stained tank top, sunglasses, and floppy hat on the dresser. She set her steel-toed boots underneath. By now she knew what would be easiest to make the trek in. She tossed her Walkman and a few tapes into her bookbag along with a change of clothes and her makeup, then she went to sleep.

For the first time in months, she woke up at the crack of dawn and dressed. She left her room to find Occasum, Donna, and Ramblin' Cat waiting outside. Ramblin' Cat was sleeping on the floor. Occasum kicked him gently awake. Once he stood up, they all hugged her.

"You can do this," said Donna. "Thank you."

Ramblin' Cat gave her one of his ironic salutes. "A pleasure to know you. I hope you come back someday."

Occasum half-smiled. "I'm your ride if you still want one." They all walked out of Sick Sustenance together, and after Princess said her goodbyes, she followed Occasum to their car. It was clearly more high-tech than Sandworm's had been. The mirrors were built directly into the body so that only a fan stuck out from the top. When they noticed her studying it, they said, "One of Rose's designs."

They drove in relative silence for an hour, and then The Wall came into view. Occasum slowed down gradually, then finally stopped. "You sure about this?" they asked. "You really think you can do this?"

Princess opened her door. "I can do this," she said. "But I'll really miss you. Hell, maybe I'll even miss dishwashing." They hugged and Princess got out and began walking.

It was a much easier walk in these boots than it had been in her heels. In what seemed like no time, The Wall was rising up before her, only twenty yards or so away. She recognized the tower rising up from it as the 43rd guard station. And she recognized the two men in it waving at her were her parent's highly trained border patrol. She waved back, wondering if they'd somehow recognized her and took off her hat and sunglasses.

$$$

Voguelle rushed to the 43rd Wall Security Tower, glittering black cape soaring along behind him. He swept through the tower and swung the door to the holding chamber open, storming in and stopped just a foot away from the soldier. The room was hot, despite being made entirely of stone, and contained one nicely cushioned chair, clearly brought in for The Grand Mage. The unconscious girl was obviously Ms. Walton-Clinton-Trump, a bit heavier, but otherwise a spitting image of her portraits.

"Who else examined the prisoner?" he asked the

officer calmly.

"Up close, only me, sir," he said. "Another officer was with me in the tower, but I retrieved the body myself and no one got a close look at her besides me. It's an honor to—"

"Do you know who this is?" Voguelle asked.

"I have my suspicions, sir," he said, wanting to seem as intelligent as possible at this important time of possible promotion.

"Call the other officer you were with."

"Steve!" the man shouted. "Steve!" After a few more shouts, another officer entered the room. "The Grand Mage—"

The door had barely closed behind the officer when Voguelle said, "My specialty is turning people into beetles, but you've served this country well, gentlemen." He focused and waved his hands about, then shouted, "Canis!" Then he clapped his hands and both men turned into dogs. The first officer's last human thoughts were how well his uniform had also transformed. It fit him just as well in this body. The second officer immediately began to wag his tail, still excited that he was meeting the Grand Mage.

"I assume your training has stuck," said Voguelle. He clapped his hands again. "Come on boys," he called and rushed back out of the room. The dogs followed. He locked the door first with the actual lock and then, as a precaution, with a quick spell. They all set off for the Gold House.

$$$

The Grand Mage Voguelle In Charge made a fittingly grand name for himself as the Bringer of Prosperity. After seeing to their daughter's deportation, Mr. and Mrs. Walton-Clinton-Trump decided it was time to stop campaigning for themselves and begin sponsoring Voguelle. He campaigned on the ticket that everyone would be guaranteed a mystical plastic fairy, no matter their income or occupation. Upon rising to the throne, he kept this promise and for a short period, the economy boomed. Factories were erected throughout the city for the purpose of creating these plastic fairies and employment went up substantially. The lower-middle class managed to not starve and Voguelle thought every home looked a bit higher class with a plastic fairy sitting in front of it or on the window sill.